## OTHER WORKS by
## CARLA MARIA VERDINO-SÜLLWOLD

Screenplay
***Raising Rufus: A Maine Love Story***

Fiction
***Top Cat: Tails of Mannahatta***
***Raising Rufus: A Maine Love Story***
***The Whaler's Bride***

Nonfiction
**We Need a Hero! *Heldentenors from Wagner's Time to the Present A Critical History***
*Method & Madness*
*Orpheus, Dionysus, and Apollo: Dialogues with the Gods & Other Essays*
*Singing in Solitude: Essays in the Arts*

Monographs
*A Bridge Between the Generations: Peter Hofmann's Rock*
*The Heldentenor in the Twentieth Century: Refining a Rare Breed*
*I Am the World: Thomas Mann and Richard Wagner: Two Early Novelle*
*Pirates in a Paper Sea: A Manifesto on Music Criticism*

Translation
*Peter Hofmann: Singing Is Like Flying* by Marieluise Müller
*The Servant of Two Masters* by Carlo Goldoni
*Peter Hofmann: Tales of A Singer's Adventures*

Internet Content
*Thomas Hampson: I Hear America Singing*
*www.pbs.org*

# BOOKENDS

## Stories of Love, Loss, and Renewal

by

Carla Maria Verdino-Süllwold

Weiala Press
An Imprint of Mannahatta M.C.
Brunswick, ME

# BOOKENDS
## Stories of Love, Loss, and Renewal


Published by Weiala Press, an imprint of Mannahatta M.C.

Front cover, text photographs by Lisa Miglietta
Rear Cover photograph by Michelle Seacord

 For information contact: Weiala Press/ Mannahatta M.C., 12 Tamarack Drive, Brunswick, ME 04011

Library of Congress Control Number: 2013923604

Library of Congress Cataloging in Publication Data available

Verdino-Süllwold, Carla Maria, 1947 –

ISBN 978-1-4675-9785-2

PRINTED IN THE UNITED STATES OF AMERICA
FIRST EDITION 2014

*To* ***Christine****,*
*for her gift of friendship and family*

*and*

*To* ***Greg****, my Theo, Jack, Magnus, Will, Gabriel, Marius, Matt, Leander, my everything – always*

## Acknowledgements

To my dear friends and best critics, **Albert H. Black, Malcolm Duffy,** cousin **Donna Pucciani,** and **Mark Wright**, for their suggestions, encouragement, and support in the development of this manuscript;

To **Malcolm Duffy** for his assistance with editing and proofreading;

And to **Lisa Miglietta** and **Michelle Seacord** for the photography.

# TABLE OF CONTENTS

# THE WEDDING

A strangled hiccup of pain escaped Olivia's lips as she dug her nails into Theo's hand. A tear rolled down her cheek, and she swayed on her feet. Theo slipped his arm around her waist to steady her, but she sank to her knees and, gripping the railing, buried her face on the velvet padding and sobbed uncontrollably.

Theo knelt beside her, rubbing her back and whispering soothingly, "Sweetheart, I know . . . I know . . . come on now. Come, Livy, let's go sit down."

Olivia raised her head and stared, red-eyed, at the waxen figure stretched still before them. "Where is she now, Theo? Where is she, do you think?" The words hissed softly from her lips.

"What?" Theo muttered in astonishment as he hoisted his wife to her feet and guided her away from the coffin. Together they made their way down the row of grieving relatives, each embrace more and more enveloping than the last.

"What will you do without your best friend?" Emilia rasped loudly.

Olivia bent down to hug the old lady. "I don't know, Mama Tesori," she replied, addressing the gnarled woman in the wheelchair by the name she had used since childhood. "I can't even imagine life without Cesca. We've been best friends for fifty years."

"The Lord does strange things," Emilia croaked in a broken voice. "But why Francesca so soon after my Antonio? Why not me? I've had a good run. It should have been my time, not hers. She had so much to live for . . ." She waved her hand in the direction of her grandchildren and son-in-law.

Letitia intervened to comfort her mother, adjusting the black shawl around her stooped shoulders. Her eyes met Livy's, and she smiled wanly. "Hey, Sis," she murmured, and stepping around her mother's wheelchair, she gave first Cesca and then Theo a hug. "We're sisters now, you know – just like you and Cesca," Letitia offered.

"Always were, Letty," Olivia replied. "All the Tesoris are my family – more than family to me."

She patted Emilia's hand and moved on down the line. As Peter Grimaldi stood up to greet them, Olivia threw herself into the widower's arms, while Theo enfolded his wife and his friend in a bear hug.

"Just the three of us now," Olivia moaned. Peter, who had been doing his best until now to be stoic, broke down noisily.

Cesca's brother Teddy edged his way over and gently urged, "Theo, Livy, come sit with us. Sit with the family."

Obediently, the Stavroses settled themselves at the end of the first row. Theo offered Olivia his neatly folded hanky, which she applied to her mascara-streaked cheeks. Sucking in a few more hoarse breaths, Olivia folded her hands in her lap and closed her eyes. To the room of devout mourners, it may have seemed as if she were praying, but she was not – not that way, anyway.

"Pray to whom? Who had done this to Cesca – Cesca, so full of life a few months ago, now vanished? For truly, the Cesca Livy knew had disappeared; the tall, handsome, confident, spirited woman, adored by her husband and sons - the soon-to-be grandmother had fled this world – fled to – fled where?" Olivia reran the anguished riddle in her head.

Faith had never played a big role in Olivia's or Theo's lives, so the relentless query was more rhetorical than not. It seemed to Livy that even for the Tesoris and Grimaldis who had never waivered in their Catholic beliefs, the Church's consolation proffered cold comfort tonight.

Olivia sighed deeply and relaxed her body into the oversized sofa cushions. She drifted, lulled by the drone of Father O'Malley's bass voice chanting the rosary. The mechanical rhythms transported Olivia to that halfway house of memory.

Nine-year-old Cesca and she were huddled under a makeshift backyard tent on a rainy summer's afternoon, sharing a picnic of peanut butter-and-jelly sandwiches with chocolate milkshakes and babbling in a secret language they had invented. When three-year-old Letty toddled over and attempted to crawl into their tent, Cesca and Livy had protested loudly, invoking Mama Tesori's aid in declaring their sanctum "off limits for babies."

The girls had been inseparable from the moment Cesca's grandfather had introduced his granddaughter to his new neighbors. When later that year, the Tesoris bought a house around the corner from Olivia's parents, the sisterhood was forged in earnest. From the age of nine, Cesca and Livy shared girlhood secrets and passions: their mania for the Beatles; their guilty obsession with certain movies – they once saw *Tom Jones* four times in a single day; their not-so-legal hobby of handicapping horse races; their love of New York City; their fascination with grand opera; their dreams of glamorous careers – Olivia was going to paint in a Paris garret, while Cesca designed haute couture – and they would take dark, handsome Frenchmen as their lovers.

And, of course, they were also going to change the world! They sneaked out on weekends to join Civil Rights marches, inventing colorful alibis for their parents' consumption. One fall night, after returning from a local demonstration, they joined their parents in Olivia's living room for a nightcap. Waxing eloquent about the latest Hitchcock film they had supposedly seen, Cesca and Livy were feeling fairly smug about their deception until their whispered giggles were interrupted by a stern shriek from Olivia's mother Rosina.

"Olivia Cantori, get in here this minute, young lady!"

Cesca in tow, Livy presented herself to her mother and Emilia, who were staring in disbelief at the small black-and-white television set on which paraded a group of chanting citizens. In the first row – the only white faces in the group – Cesca and

Livy proudly marched behind the banner extolling "Integrated Housing for the Fourth Ward."

"You lied, young lady!" Rosina sputtered. "You're grounded!"

"Oh, Rosie," Cesca's father Antonio soothed. "There are worse places they could have been. Cheers!" he smiled, clinking cocktail glasses and diffusing the crisis.

"Dear old Daddy Tesori," Livy recalled. "How I miss him, too!" Her lips shaped a phrase silently: "What a prince!"

Theo leaned over to catch her words, thinking she was addressing him. Instead, Livy nestled back into the protective warmth of the overstuffed pillows and, without opening her eyes, smiled from a faraway place.

She felt Theo's fingers jab her ribs gently as the assembly responded in a rousing "Amen." The rosary was over, and Father O'Malley had stepped away from the podium to offer his condolences to the family. When he reached Olivia and Theo, he looked puzzled, searching his memory for recognition. Letitia came to his rescue, "Father, this is Cesca's best friend, Livy, and her husband."

“I do remember. You were her maid of honor, weren’t you?”

“Yes,” Olivia replied softly, “and Aaron’s godmother. You married Cesca and Peter,” she added.

“I did, indeed! A wedding I’ll never forget,” the priest chuckled, shaking his head. The ironic emphasis in his tone brought an involuntary smile to Olivia’s lips.

“It was kind of unforgettable,” she acceded.

“I’ve performed thousands of marriage ceremonies in the last thirty years, but nothing like that one,” O’Malley grinned. “Wasn’t the most auspicious start, but where there’s love, anything’s possible,” he sermonized, excusing himself to continue his pastoral rounds.

Olivia and Theo sat back down, and Livy slipped her hand into her husband’s and again closed her eyes, trying to transport herself from the suffocating parlor with its flickering candles and cloying floral perfume. To make the torturous time remaining at the wake pass quickly, she let her mind flee the present and wander through a labyrinth of memory.

Cesca's wedding, August 10, 1972, was a day that had begun with delirious anticipation and had played itself out like a Robert Altman film – a day that had rewritten a joyous, meticulously planned romantic script as theatre-of-the-absurd – a day whose scars had seared – and yes, redeemed - Peter and Francesca's lives.

*****

Livy had arrived at the Tesori home early that afternoon to help Cesca dress and to share some private time before the ceremony. Cesca looked radiant, her chestnut hair sculpted in a bouffant style, her salon makeup and nails perfect.

"You look beautiful!" Livy exclaimed. "Peter is one lucky guy! You nervous, Cesca?"

"A little," her friend confided. "But Mom and Noni have planned everything so perfectly it'll be fine. Were you nervous when you and Theo got married?" she asked, undermining her show of confidence.

"No, but we were probably too dumb," Livy replied, thinking of her own wedding three years before. "We knew we were pissing off all the relatives, and we just didn't care. We did exactly what we wanted," she laughed, recalling how Theo and she had defied their families not only in their decision to marry, but also to marry without the blessing of the Church.

"It was a lovely ceremony," Cesca recalled of the candlelight Quaker wedding, "- so simple and so real. Today is going to be more of a production," she winced.

"Better get on with it then," Olivia remarked. "Here, put this on – something old, you know," she said, handing Cesca a tiny gold pinkie ring. "It was my grandma's."

A tear glistened in the corner of Cesca's eye as she slipped on the ring and hugged her friend. "We'd better get dressed."

An hour later the Tesori house had filled with noisy laughter as the bridesmaids smoothed their floral chiffon gowns and checked the tilt of their picture hats in the mirror. The photographer was gathering up his gear and making his way downstairs and out to his car.

"Ready, girls?" Mama Tesori called up. "The limos are here. Cesca, let me see you," she called from the foot of the stairs. "Noni and I are going to go on ahead. Give us five minutes and then start," she commanded with the intensity of a domestic general.

Precisely five minutes later the six attendants obeyed the matriarchal order, sweeping out onto the manicured, sunlit suburban lawn. Cesca appeared at the top of the stairs in her ivory satin V-necked gown with its slim skirt and fan-shaped train. She looked understated and elegant, radiant in a quiet, self-assured way. She paused and inhaled imperceptibly; then she whispered to Livy, "Let's go." Letitia handed her the white rose bouquet; Olivia gathered up the train, and all three descended.

"Here come my girls," Antonio beamed. Livy spied the tear in his fading blue eyes and fought back the catch in her own throat. What she would have given for this kind, sweet man to have been her dad, but then, in a way, he always had been . . .

"You look like a fairy princess, Chessie," he stammered awkwardly, giving his daughter a peck on the cheek and helping her down the front steps to the waiting white limousine.

At St. John's the massive carved oak portals were drawn open to reveal the pews that were already overflowing. As the bridal party made their way into the vestibule, Livy peered down the aisle. The altar was brimming with white lilies and roses. She spotted Theo seated in the second pew on the left with her parents, Rosina and Sal, just behind the Tesoris. Her mother's black knit dress and mantilla seemed more appropriate for a funeral, but then Mama Rose had not worn any other color for the last five years since her papa had died, and today was no exception. She cut a sharp contrast to Emilia Tesori in her ice-blue satin suit, plumed lampshade hat, and dangling pearl earrings.

On seeing the bride enter, Peter's cousin, Rick, strode down the aisle to greet them. "Looks like we are all set, if you are," he volunteered. "Pete is getting pretty antsy back there. He's asked Henny six times if he has the ring," he quipped.

"Is everyone here then?" Antonio asked.

"Well, everyone except Aunt Tilda, but Pete doesn't think she's coming, so – "

Antonio hesitated. Matilda Grimaldi had been the thorn in their sides throughout the wedding preparations. Widowed ten months before, she had insisted that Peter and Francesca postpone the wedding for another year. "Proper mourning demanded that show of propriety," she had insisted. "No self-respecting girl would break that rule, and no loving son would leave his widowed mother alone so soon."

When the Tesoris demurred, citing the elaborate prepaid arrangements and when Cesca had pleaded with Peter not to delay their happiness, he had stepped in firmly and silenced his mother's protests. He was twenty-eight years old, and he was going to begin his own life, and there was nothing she could say that would change that. If she felt it was disrespectful, she could stay at home.

"I hope she has," Cesca whispered to Livy as she drew her veil over her face and signaled to Rick that they were, indeed, ready. Turning to face the apse, she slipped her arm through her father's, straightened her shoulders, and smiled as the ushers unfurled the white runner. Beaming broadly, Father O'Malley stepped out onto the altar and nodded to the organist in the choir loft.

The wedding party had their backs turned away from the open portico as the first majestic *Lohengrin* chords drowned out the screeching brakes of a gold stretch limousine sliding into the last reserved parking space in front of the church. The chauffeur threw the door open and before he could offer his assistance to the occupant, a petite, platinum blonde woman wearing a black sequined suit and a pillbox hat from which flowed a long chiffon widow's veil flew from the car and clattered up the stone steps of the church in her spike heels. The sun sparkled off the large faceted rock on her left hand. Antonio wheeled around just as Matilda Grimaldi swept into the foyer.

The groom and best man had just made their appearances at the altar. Too late! The organist had just given the cue to the choir, who rose poised to sing the *Brautgemacht*. The congregation had risen to their feet and turned toward the back of the nave.

Looking stricken, Rick intervened. "Aunt Tilda, come," he whispered as smoothly as he could. "You're just in time. Let me seat you," he said, offering his arm.

"I want Peter!" she shrieked, giving her nephew an unceremonious shove. Matilda swung around to face her rival. A Fury framed in the Gothic arch of the nave's entryway, she etched a garish silhouette, surrounded by a sea of expectant faces. "I want my son to escort me!"

White-lipped, Rick tried again. "Auntie, please. Peter's already at the altar."

"*Putana*!" she hissed at Cesca. "Have you no decency? My poor Aldo not yet cold in his grave! God will punish you," she rasped through contorted lips.

"Mrs. Grimaldi, please," Cesca sputtered with as much authority as she could muster." "Please," she added more helplessly as she dissolved into tears.

Antonio put his arm around his daughter's shoulder. "Chessie, please don't cry. Don't, darling. You'll ruin your makeup," he trailed off as Cesca collapsed sobbing on his shoulder.

The momentary lull in the cacophony of battle caused the organist, who had stopped mid-chord, to resume the march with a meaningful vengeance. The guests who had frozen, then sat, now stood again, and like some marionettes in a bizarre choreographic sequence turned first to Father O'Malley for guidance and then back to the vestibule.

Trembling and stamping her foot, Matilda summoned another crescendo of hysteria. "I want Peter! NOW! I am his mother!" she howled.

*Heilige Braut* the sopranos of the choir warbled in helpless, confused counterpoint.

Pivoting dramatically, Matilda was not prepared for what confronted her. There, inches from her now livid face, was that of her son Peter. His blue eyes blazed with anger. His ashen face matched the crisp summer dinner jacket he wore. Without a word, he locked his arm around his mother's elbow and strode down the aisle. The stunned harpy's feet barely grazed the bridal carpet; her black veil trailed behind her like a wake. In a matter of seconds she found herself thrust into the front pew opposite the wide-eyed Tesoris.

Only then did Peter emit an audible sigh. He adjusted his jacket, straightened his boutonniere, and resumed his place at the altar beside his best man. Father O'Malley, wisely believing the best course lay in forging ahead, signaled once more to the organist, who abruptly silenced the choir and sounded the processional opening once again.

"Go, go, go," whispered Letty, pushing the first bridesmaids into line.

Like sleepwalkers emerging from a dream, the girls began to process down the aisle. Livy hastily thrust some tissues at Cesca, who now stood still and silent. not fully comprehending the significance of the tragicomedy she had just witnessed. Wiping away the rivulets of mascara from under her eyes, Francesca lowered her veil once more.

Livy handed Cesca the bouquet and stepped into the procession. By the time she reached the altar rail and turned to welcome the bride, Cesca was again smiling – almost radiantly – on her father's arm. Antonio lifted his daughter's veil, kissed her gently, and slipped into the pew beside his wife whose stony features told him immediately that Emilia was doing her utmost to hold in check the rage welling up inside her. Silently and supportively, he took his wife's hand.

Livy paused in her reverie. She could recall very little else about the actual service. Everyone had seemed propelled in a daze. The mass droned on; the litany washed over them. The congregation stood and knelt and stood again. Vows were exchanged, the rings received, the final proclamation sealed with a kiss before the raucously joyous Widor *Recessional* burst from the organ loft. Only then did most of the guests break into smiles, relieved, it seemed, to reach the dénouement of this theatre-of-the-absurd production.

Father O'Malley prudently hastened everyone through the receiving line. Somehow Cesca maintained a polite and placid countenance while Peter still struggled for a vestige of calm. Only when they had escaped into the limousine did Cesca break down again and hide her face on Peter's shoulder.

"My tux is going to need a good dry-cleaning," he quipped with as much sangfroid as he could summon.

****

Half smiling, Livy opened her eyes as if emerging from that long ago memory and glanced sideways at Peter. He seemed oddly composed given the lengthy battle of the past two years with Cesca's cancer. "But, then, that was Peter," she thought. That outrageous day thirty-five years ago he had been forced to make a choice, and he had chosen, unequivocally, without a moment's hesitation, the woman he loved whose corpse now lay still before them. Livy threaded her arm through Theo's and gave his hand a little squeeze. Perhaps she and Cesca had been lucky after all – husbands who loved them and whom they loved, lives filled with meaning and caring.

Livy felt Theo pressure her elbow, lifting her to her feet. The funeral director was bidding them to take their last farewells. Olivia and Theo preceded the immediate family. Theo kept a firm grip on his wife's waist to steady her as they approached the casket. Livy knelt one more time and, with trembling fingers, softly patted her friend's cold hand. She stood up, stepped back, and looked hard at the waxen form with its grimly set lips, its visage etched in steely, sad lines. This was not the face that Cesca had worn in life. Yet, Livy told herself that in an odd way, she did recognize that look.

Livy stood up and glanced one more time at the silent sleeper, and then it struck her! The expression she saw spoke of regret, disbelief, even anger at a life cut short, plans unrealized, hopes dashed in their prime. This imposter who lay before her in the heartless metal box wore a mask – a mask which terrified Livy with its denial of all the warm vitality with which Cesca had lived.

But then in an instant, Livy knew where she had seen this unfamiliar face before. It was the sad, crestfallen countenance that Cesca had inadvertently revealed at her marriage. Like a missing bookend, this funeral mirrored Cesca's wedding day thirty-five years ago when dreams seemed to have deserted her and feast had nearly turned to fiasco.

# BRAVE LADIES

Absentmindedly Caroline fluffed the foam of her cappuccino with a teaspoon and tried to focus on her cousins' animated chatter. Instead, her eyes wandered up to the frescoed medallions on the gilded ceiling and down again to the winged classical nude sculptures that flanked the Palmer House Lobby Bar. The late afternoon light reflected by the huge candelabras ricocheted off the mosaic columns. There was so much glitter that for a moment she imagined herself in an ancient tomb until the rumble of the passing El brought her back to herself.

"Caro, are you OK?" Donatella interrupted.

"Oh, yes, just tired from the long train ride. I didn't sleep much in the roomette last night."

"Well, if you had flown, instead -" Donatella chided. Caroline suppressed a reply before Donatella's sister came to the rescue.

"Oh, Dona, you know how Caro feels about flying ever since 9/11," Lydia intervened. "We're just glad you came. It's been so long since the three of us have been together," she soothed in her musical voice.

"Yes, it has," Caroline agreed. "So much has happened," she trailed off quietly.

Lydia tried again to boost the mood. "Remember when we were all teaching in the city and the six of us would get together on the weekends for brunch and then go to the Art Institute or Symphony Hall or head out to the zoo or Wrigley Field?"

"And then we would go back to your house, Caro," Dona joined in, "and Jack would whip up a delicious meal, and we'd drink Chianti and talk until midnight."

"Yes, I do," Caroline replied wistfully. "How I miss that!" She almost said, "How I miss HIM," but she had promised herself not to dampen the reunion with her grief.

Had it really been two decades since she had called Chicago home, she wondered. All three cousins had come to the Midwest in teaching jobs, their husbands in tow. They had been young, restless, and fearless, eager for any challenge.

Caroline and Jack had spent almost eight years at the Academy in Lake Forest – he as business manager and she as arts-department chair, and though they were New Yorkers at heart, they had learned to embrace Second City. As an only child, Caroline liked living close to her twin cousins. It was like having the sisters for whom she had always wished. But after a while, Wall Street had called to Jack; they had moved back to New York and then eventually retired to Maine, where in a frightful, unpitying instant, Caro's life had changed forever.

She emerged from her reverie to see Lydia and Donatella exchanging meaningful glances, but before they could speak, Caroline shifted the focus. "How is Jon doing, Liddy? Is he doing OK with the chemo?"

"Well, he's exhausted most of the time and pretty depressed. I know he hates not being able to go to the office. On good days he'll do a little editing from home – an hour or two at the computer – and then he's finished. I come home from work, and he's asleep in front of the TV."

"And you know how he used to rail about watching the boob tube," added Donatella, trying to project amusement, only succeeding in bitter irony.

Caro hesitated a moment and then decided to ask the question that had formed on her lips. "What do the doctors tell you? What's the next step?" Lydia bit her lip and looked away as Dona, with her characteristic unflinching candor, took up the challenge.

"They say it's fifty-fifty that it won't come back or metastasize." She spoke matter-of-factly. "They've removed the tumor in the lung this time, but if it grows back, they may not be able to . . . "

Caro processed the ominous words in silence. "May not be able to what?"

"Save him." Lydia's voice was a whisper. "They don't think it's advisable to operate a second time."

"Well, we're not there yet, Sis," Dona urged. "Let's not go there now," she repeated lamely.

Caro attempted to redirect the conversation. "It must really be hard on you, Liddy. With Teri in Europe and you still teaching – I mean the house, the job, Jon. Has Teri considered coming home for a while," she inquired of her cousin's daughter, "or can you pay for some help?"

"I wouldn't ask Teri," Lydia softly replied. "She's young; she's in the middle of her master's; she . . ." She feebly abandoned the rationale, "and I did think of taking a leave of absence from teaching, but I really can't afford to."

"They've gone through most of their savings with this," Dona explained. "You know how miserable parochial school medical insurance is. God damn!" She veered off course. "They ask you to put up with substandard wages and bratty kids. You give two hundred percent, and what do you get when YOU need something more?"

Caro chose to ignore Dona's rant, though she knew from her own decades of teaching that her cousin was not exaggerating. Luckily for Caro, Jack had rescued her when the classroom no longer felt like her true métier; he had supported and, indeed, encouraged her career change and watched her flourish as a journalist and novelist.

When she fell sick from pneumonia that winter twenty years ago – pneumonia brought on by frustration and stress, overwork and underappreciation - Jack had insisted she tender her resignation at the end of the school year. "I can't watch you destroy yourself. You've got too much else to give," he had urged.

"Always generous to a fault," Caroline thought of Jack, and suddenly she was overwhelmed with a nameless guilt - for Jack, who had shouldered so much throughout their marriage, yes – but even more for her own financially comfortable widowhood and her cousin's hardship.

She reached out awkwardly and touched Lydia's hand. "Can I help?"

She was a little surprised at the vehemence of the retort. "Of course not! We'll manage. We always have," Lydia snapped.

"I didn't mean . . ." Caro broke off. "You and Jon have always been such an indomitable team. Remember when you were eight months pregnant with Teri and he lost his job at Ticknor's? You taught all day and did telemarketing at night until the baby came. And then Jon took over, taking any work that came his way until he finally found an editorship again. And you know what amazed Jack and me the most? You never lost your cool. You were so serene and unruffled. I'd have been a basket case," Caro confided.

Lydia only nodded, content, it seemed, to let this subject go. They all fell silent again. But Caroline somehow could not leave the discussion unfinished. "I know I should shut up," she chastised herself, "but what about your father's will? Didn't Uncle Sal leave you both with some means to help now?"

Donatella snorted ambiguously. “After two years in St. Francis, there wasn’t anything left,” she added.

“Was it that long?” Caroline asked. “It seems only yesterday that Jack and I came out to visit you. Uncle Sal was still with you and Alistair. Aunt Mae had just died.”

“That was almost four years ago, Coz,” Dona said flatly. “He went downhill pretty quickly after that. It wasn’t just the Parkinson’s. He had dementia, too. Did you know?” Caro nodded in the affirmative.

“Funny,” Donatella continued, “all his life he was saddled with taking care of her; he never really had a moment to call his own. He was always at her beck and call, always trying to keep her happy – a woman who didn’t know the definition of the word!” Donatella said irritably. “He lived in fear of another drinking binge or suicide attempt. He tiptoed through fifty years of marriage and then in six short months she wasted away and died, and he was completely lost without her. When Alistair and I went down to New Orleans to get him, we were horrified at how much weight he had lost and how” – she hesitated searching for the word – “how vacant he seemed.”

"I think I understand," Caro said softly. "You don't invest all those years in a relationship and not feel adrift when it disappears."

"But Dad was always so intellectually alert, curious – at least with us he was," Lydia mused. "The dementia was so sudden."

"Maybe he wanted to forget," Caroline suggested softly. "Maybe it was just too much to imagine a different kind of life at his age."

"He deserved a better one," Dona insisted. "But he grew so bitter. He was angry at Liddy and me for making him move into the assisted living apartment at St. Francis. He wanted to live with one of us, but that just wouldn't have worked." Lydia bit her lip and said nothing as Dona continued vehemently. "I wasn't going to put that kind of strain on Alistair and my marriage."

"No need to apologize, Dona. You did what you thought best," Caro consoled. "It would have ended there sooner or later. Getting old sucks no matter how you approach it. Be glad you have Alistair and Jon," Caroline told her cousins, trying to sound upbeat.

"For now," Lydia murmured.

"Yes, for now, but that's something!" Caroline became insistent. "Believe me, that IS something to hold on to, to cherish, every single minute that you can - to make the little things so big, so important that they never leave your memory. How I wish –" and she left off suddenly.

She felt a lump rise in her throat and her eyes flood with tears. Glancing around in awkward embarrassment, Caroline was relieved to notice the Lobby Bar had pretty well cleared out. She signaled for the waiter, who promptly responded by bringing the check.

Caroline handed him her credit card but surprised her cousins by adding, "Can you please bring us three glasses of Asti Spumante and put it all on the card?" Dona and Lydia exchanged quizzical looks. "It's not often we are all together. It is a special occasion," Caro explained.

The waiter returned with the flutes. Dona attempted to lift the mood. "Do you remember the games we used to play at Noni and Grandpa's?" she ventured.

"Brave Ladies," Lydia smiled. "That was our favorite."

Caroline brightened at the memory. "We would argue about which heroines we each got to be. Do you remember what role you always wanted to play, Liddy?" she asked.

"Marie Antoinette. I loved acting the Queen. I'd make a train out of the bedspread and have you two carry it for me down the stairs and outside to the guillotine."

"And you made an endless death speech," Dona twitted her.

"About how you had loved Louis and your people and your little white dog," Caro laughed. "Your farewell to the dog went on longer than your goodbye to your husband. What was the dog's name?"

"Fifi," Lydia giggled. "Dona and I had always wanted a puppy, but Mom was allergic," she added by way of justification.

"And I would pretend to be Joan of Arc," Donatella recalled. "I would gallop through the garden on a broomstick yelling 'To arms for France and the Dauphin!' And I'd crown Liddy king and then you, Caro, would be Cauchon and arrest me and tie me to Grandpa's fig tree. And I would call on my Voices to save me, but they would abandon me." Lydia seemed immersed in the memory.

"Yeah, they almost did for real," Caroline remembered the irony. "Thanks to the brush fire Dona and I started!"

"Oh, my God was Noni angry!" Dona chuckled. "She came running out, screaming '*Vado amazzarle tutti*' and doused the flames.

"A little cinema verité," Caroline joked.

"And, you? Who was your brave lady, Caro?" Lydia asked.

"Heloïse, don't you remember? Heloïse and Abelard were my heroes."

"Not exactly an action movie," Dona teased. "Not even a death scene."

"No, contemplative, introspective, but brave and beautiful just the same." Caroline took a sip of her champagne. "They suffered for love – that's the hardest, I think."

The quiet, determined certainty of Caro's last remark plunged the cousins into a long silence before Lydia spoke up. She raised her flute and extended it in a toast. "Here's to the loves we've lost." She turned to her sister, who likewise raised her glass.

"To the heroines we dreamt of becoming," Donatella smiled nostalgically.

Caroline paused a moment and then solemnly clinked each of her cousin's glasses. "Better yet. Let's drink to the brave ladies we have become."

# A GRAIN OF SAND

"It's just that it is all so sudden, honey," Christina said softly. With a sigh she reached across the kitchen table and took her daughter's outstretched hands in her own. "But, of course, I'm happy for you, Laura, and Eddie."

Laura smiled wanly, stood up and began to clear the dinner table. Christina, lost in thought, did not stir. "A wedding," she repeated to herself, still trying to process her daughter's unexpected announcement. "So much to do," she murmured.

"Not that much, really, Mom," Laura replied, trying to sound nonchalant. "We're just going to have a very small service at the Unitarian Church and invite only a few people. We want to keep it simple."

Christina remained silent, not wanting to share with Laura all the memories that raced through her mind. Hadn't she uttered pretty much the same words to her own mother more than thirty-five years ago when she and Magnus had made the impetuous decision to wed while they were still in college. No amount of pleading or sweet-talking could calm Peppina's hysteria at the idea of Christina's leaving the nest, marrying a Norwegian engineering student in a Quaker ceremony no less! Christina recalled the long night of noisy argument which ended as it always did between them – with Peppina's bitter silence.

She did not want to replay that scene tonight with Laura. She rose wearily to her feet and began to load the dishwasher. "We can talk about your plans tomorrow, hon. Does Eddie want to come to dinner? We can all talk," Christina asked in a conciliatory way. "How I wish your father were here (she almost said) to help me get through this," but she voiced a different sentiment. "He would be happy for you – and proud."

Laura nodded sadly and gave her mother an awkward hug. "I know, Mom. I miss Daddy, too. I know it has been hard for you, but Eddie and I will still be around after we graduate. We won't abandon you."

Christina checked the skeptical reply forming on her lips. "Do not play this scene like Peppina," she chided herself. "That would be nice, but you have your own lives. Let's just focus on the wedding for now." And she gave Laura a kiss on the cheek.

“I’m exhausted. I’m going to turn in. We’ll discuss it all tomorrow night.”

****

When Christina came home from work the next afternoon, Laura was not home. There was a note on the refrigerator that she and Eddie had gone to the movies. Christina was almost relieved to put off their talk. She was frazzled from a long day of teaching – five classes of nonplussed teenagers. Even her A.P. Lit class, which once gave her such joy, now seemed apathetic, cynically unconvinced of the value of reading William Blake. “What’s the use of studying some old schizophrenic who heard voices?” one sullen young man had challenged her today. “It’s not going to help me get into business school.”

“No, perhaps not, but it will help you to do something even better,” Christina had replied coolly. “It will teach you to see beyond yourself, your narrow little world!”

Then she began to quote the verse she and Magnus had read at their wedding. *To see a World in a Grain of Sand/ And a Heaven in a Wild Flower* she recited before breaking off in exasperation. She turned quickly to the blackboard to hide the stinging tears of frustration. Perhaps she did not hear the young man’s apology.

Since Magnus had died, the challenge of shaping young minds had lost some of its thrill, but then, so had most other things. It had been six years now since she had received the terrifying phone call from the hospital. Magnus - strapping, tall, blond, seemingly invincible - had, at forty-nine, been felled by a massive heart attack as he sat at his office desk. For six years she had plodded through each day praying for the strength to make it to nightfall. As a single parent now, she had thrown whatever tenderness and hope that was left in her desolate heart into raising Laura, who as a fourteen-year-old child had been bright, driven, headstrong, and rebellious.

It seemed to Christina that it had taken all her energy to insure that Laura made it to adulthood without becoming a train wreck. And now just when Laura, a junior at Rutgers, had finally seemed to be finding herself as a journalism major and a blossoming, beautiful young woman, when a measure of tranquility had returned to their lives, Laura had fallen headlong in love with Eddie Parker. And now she would be leaving home, marrying, going off on her own to what and where Christina did not know. Where would her daughter and husband get the money to live? Neither she nor Eddie's parents would be able to contribute much to the newlyweds while they finished their degrees.

"We'll get jobs, Mom. Don't worry. You worry too much," Laura had blithely reassured her.

"Ah, to be that young again – so free of the inhibitions of practicality," Christina sighed. "Well, if Laura wasn't going to think sensibly, I will have to," Christina told herself resolutely. "The first thing is this wedding. Small or not, we need a caterer, and she needs a dress. Unless she can use mine? Would Laura want to?" They were about the same size though Laura was a little taller and still had the willowy slenderness of youth.

Christina went into her bedroom and opened the hope chest at the foot of the four-poster. Almost reverently she lifted out the garment bag with the carefully folded gown. She spread the empress-style ivory satin dress on the bed and surveyed it critically. It was understated, plain even, suitable for Magnus' and her Friends ceremony. The sleeves were long and tight fitting; the neckline was cut in a graceful, modest scoop. From the high princess waist the skirt flowed into elegant pleats. Christina held it up to her shoulders and took in the effect in the full-length mirror.

"Yes, with a few alterations it could do very nicely." Peppina could tailor it. The old woman still loved to sew. It would give her pleasure, and it would save them a fair sum.

Smiling at her ingenuity, Christina brought the gown into Laura's room and left it on her daughter's bed. They would decide in the morning.

****

Christina sat with her hands folded in her lap as Peppina bent intently over the dress spread out on the sewing table. The old woman - her skin like parchment creased into a thousand folds - peered at the tiny stitches she was removing from the neckline.

"*Così*," she asked, indicating with her fingers the amount of fabric she would trim from the bodice. "*Vuoi fare un poco più scollata*?"

"*Si, Mama, per piacere. Sai come i giovinetti d'oggi sono.*"

"*Sicuro*," Peppina replied disapprovingly.

It never ceased to amaze Christina how the almost eighty-year-old woman with pale and fading eyes could still sew so beautifully. But, of course, why not? It had been her trade, something she had been raised to do, when she had sewn vestments and altar cloths for her cousin, Padre Giovanni, pastor of the Romanesque church atop the mountain in those distant Calabrian hills.

Christina remembered her own girlhood when Peppina had made all her and her sister's clothes. She had often wished she could buy dresses the way her friends did – have styles that were more in mode – but Peppina would not hear of it! Not the frugal immigrant woman, the sturdy peasant, who had tended her father's goats, helped out in the tavern he owned, and left school at twelve to make her way as a seamstress. Then she had shipped the long passage across the Atlantic to enter into a loveless marriage with a young man from San Donato. Together they had reared three children - Christina, the middle child. And now, Peppina, widowed too for ten years, lived alone, her only solace her two girls, her son, and her grandchildren.

A mouth full of pins projected like quills from her thin, sternly set lips, as Peppina's gnarled fingers removed the last stitch and prepared to adjust the décolletage.

*"Grazie, Mama, m'aiutai molto. Sai questo matrimonio costa tanto e non ho il denaro senza Magnus."*

Peppina grunted and let the pins excuse her for wisely keeping silent on the subject of Magnus – a subject to which, despite thirty-five years, she had never warmed. Having marked the new neckline, the old woman replaced the remaining pins in their cushion, sighed, gathered up the billowing satin, and placed the dress over Christina's outstretched arms.

"*Laura sarà bella,*" she assured her daughter, "*come te,*" and then, in a rare gesture of affection, she patted Christina's cheek.

Christina smiled and let the gown drop to her lap where it lay a suspended link between the two women. After a moment of silence, Christina held up the dress to survey the bodice. As she did so, she felt a rustling of something falling into her lap. She reached down, and there was a small cluster of flecks – tiny, yellowed, desiccated, aging grains of rice.

Gently, Christina lifted several of these specks up and let them fall through her fingers as through a sieve to her lap once again. Like the rain which comes too late to revive the withered plant, a tear fell on the tiny flakes.

"*Guarda, Mama,*" Christina whispered. The old woman smiled her toothless grin; her pallid blue eyes, watery with age, filled with something like real emotion.

"*E un segno di Dio,*" Peppina declared.

Christina remained silent. Not waiting for a reply, Peppina took back the dress and inserted the pinned neckline under the presser foot of the ancient Singer machine. Slowly, she started the pedal and rounded each curve with precision. As she had almost completed the circle, she felt the unexpected pressure of Christina's hand on her arm.

"*Cessi.*" Their eyes met, and Christina lifted several granules of rice and carefully inserted them in the tiny, open pocket of the neckline. "*Va bene ora. E un regalo per Laura.*"

As Peppina's sewing machine hummed the final inches, the words of Blake's poem crept back into Christina's mind: *To see a World in a Grain of Sand/ And a Heaven in a Wild Flower,/Hold Infinity in the palm of your hand . .*

Peppina finished sewing and with a terse smile of satisfaction handed her daughter the dress. "*Finita. Spero che Laura la piace.*"

"*Si, speriamo, Mama.*" Christina rose, collected the dress and her purse, and then bent over to kiss her mother's cheek. "*Grazie tanto, Mama. Ti chiamo. Arrivaderci.*" Christina took her leave more hurriedly than her mother would have wished.

"*Eh! Rimani. Cosa a mangiare?*" the old woman called after her daughter.

Outside at her car, Christina settled the gown on the back seat smoothing it as if it were a priceless treasure. She folded the arms across the bodice and patted the new neckline. She got into the driver's seat, and as she started the engine, she flipped on the radio.

An aching melancholy of the sonorous organ emerged from the speakers. She leaned her head back against the seat and closed her eyes. It was Albinoni's *Adagio in G for Organ and Strings*. In the six years since Magnus had departed, she had forsaken her belief in mere coincidence. This had been one of Magnus' favorite compositions, something which always elicited from him deep emotion.

She listened to the mournful organ's sobbing; then the swell of strings replying; this dialogue continuing in arching phrases, the organ lament, the strings challenging the loss of transcendence. At the final elegiac crescendo, Christina opened her eyes and sat bolt upright. The line that completed Blake's stanza – the line that had eluded her yesterday in class and just a short while before – swept into her head. She recited it aloud: *To see a World in a Grain of Sand/ And a Heaven in a Wild Flower,/ Hold Infinity in the palm of your hand,/ And Eternity in an hour.*

She, Christina, and her Magnus had known that hour, and now it was Laura's to hold.

# LEONARDO . . . ON THE BEACH

India shaded her eyes from the late autumn sun and stopped in her tracks. Beads of water cascaded like diamonds from the Lincoln Center fountain splashing playfully onto the black marble rim. But it was not the shimmering droplets that had arrested her advance. No, it was the sight of a darkly handsome young man seated on the edge of the fountain.

There he was – a tall, almost gangly, olive-skinned man of about thirty-five, his longish straight black hair flopping carelessly onto his brow and creeping over the collar of his white linen shirt which he wore open at the neck to reveal a braided gold chain. Despite the glare, India focused on his eyes which were a close-set deep chocolate brown. Framing that unmistakable aquiline nose, they gave him the intent look of an Etruscan warrior just as his lips curled ever so faintly in an archaic smile.

This air of seductive mystery in and of itself might have riveted India, but in truth, it was not the beguiling and familiar mask which made her pause. No, it was the jaunty placement of the sitter's arm – draped nonchalantly around the shoulders of a well-muscled youth who leaned in against him, basking in the afternoon sun.

"Renzo?" she asked herself. "That couldn't be Renzo." The brilliance of the light was deceiving her. And before she could comfort herself with that thought, the pair got up and walked quickly away in the direction of the opera house.

India followed. She had a ticket for *La Bohème* that night. Will was out of town on business, but she had decided to go anyway. It was Pavarotti and Scotto – by no means her favorite cast – but she had concluded that it was a more enjoyable way to pass the evening than waiting alone for her husband's return from California. As she swung through the revolving doors and merged into the crowd milling in the lobby, she caught another glimpse of the young men, but then their faces were lost in the maze.

Minutes later the ushers drew back the velvet ropes and the crowd surged in. India climbed the grand staircase to the balcony, scanning the crowds for another quick look. As the chimes sounded *Mi chiamano Mimì*, she reluctantly took her seat, resigned to the fact that her "sighting" of Renzo had been an apparition. So by the time the curtain did fall ecstatically on the first act duet, all traces of bittersweet memory had been erased from India's mind.

She had been hallucinating. Of course, it wasn't Renzo. Why would it be after almost a decade? Hadn't she heard that, after their breakup, he had moved away from New Jersey and headed to San Francisco to frame a new life? Surely, this intriguing, obviously involved couple had nothing to do with her old love. India shook her head and almost laughed aloud at her foolishness as she cued up at the bar to treat herself to a glass of champagne. Flute in hand, she dialed Will in California (it was only dinner time there), but his phone went directly to voice mail. She left a disappointed message and headed up the stairs to reclaim her seat.

As she rounded the turn from the Grand Tier to the Balcony, she came to an abrupt halt. There on the landing above her stood the Etruscan. This time he saw her as well. He was alone without the youth at the fountain. In the soft light of the crystalline sconces, he seemed older than before. His eyes were rimmed with crow's feet that turned down at the corners in a sad expression, and his hair seemed badly cut and tousled. There was a consciously bohemian air to his appearance, but there was no mistaking who it was. For an instant India's and Renzo's eyes locked. Neither spoke as

India forced herself to climb the stairs and silently slip by his motionless figure.

****

The day was dazzlingly bright, and India was impatient to get on the road, but her mother kept waylaying her with one admonition after another.

"IN-DI-A." She pronounced her daughter's name deliberately in a way that always made India cringe. Antoinette had been swept away by *Passage to India* when she was pregnant – one of the many sad flights of romantic fancy with which the poor woman who had never left West New York, New Jersey, indulged herself. Now she said it with all the emphasis of a dowager queen addressing a wayward princess.

"India, be very careful. It's a rented car, and your father can't afford an accident on his insurance."

"Yes, Mother."

"And be home no later than midnight. I can't wait up all night."

"You don't have to, Mother." Antoinette merely snorted.

India made it to the front door with her beach bag in hand. "Yes, Mother."

"And be sure that your body makeup doesn't run."

India groaned. Her mother had insisted that if she was going to wear a bikini, she must cover her "imperfections." India fully intended to shower away the sticky beige cream in the locker room before donning her swimsuit.

"Uh-huh," India muttered. "See you," she added, closing the door hastily behind her. It was only after she had turned the key in the ignition, put on a tape of Franco Corelli, and pulled out of the driveway a little too emphatically that she breathed a sigh of relief. She had managed to escape, and she was on her way to the Jersey Shore to spend the day with Renzo.

Her heart throbbed with excitement. For the past year she and Renzo had dated every Saturday night – mostly in New York City where Renzo loved to play the sophisticate, introducing India to restaurants, theatres, and amusements she had never experienced. They ate at Sardi's and had cocktails at the Playboy Club. They swooned over Corelli and Tebaldi at the Met and sat in orchestra seats for *Cabaret*. This, however, would be the first time they would spend the entire day together, completely alone, on Renzo's home turf.

India's beau had graduated as a chemist and fled the paternal nest, choosing a cozy shore cottage in Leonardo to create his bachelor pad. Until today, he had been almost secretive about it, so when he did ask India to visit him, she felt the significance of the gesture, and she attached to it great romantic expectations.

For, in truth, India Bertolini was in love with Lorenzo Almansi – deeply in love, her first serious adult romance. And all the stars seemed to be perfectly aligned for this fairy tale. After all, both she and Renzo were of Italian parentage, but more than simply Italian. Indeed, they were Sicilian – which, in fact, Antoinette would proudly emphasize was an entirely different breed. They were Catholic – well, their families were more than they – but they both understood the context that had at once shaped them and repelled them. Renzo, the youngest of nine children, had a twin sister who was a Dominican nun, and he himself had flirted with the seminary before opting for a master's degree in something far more empirical. Though he made his living among test tubes and petri dishes, Renzo had the soul of a poet. It was his secret longing for a bohemian existence that drew him to India, an art major at Sarah Lawrence, whose dream had been to flee to a Paris garret upon her graduation.

Since meeting Renzo, that desire had begun to wane. Instead of yearning for a view of Sacre Coeur, she began to wish for a modest Upper West Side flat where she and Renzo could live, love, work, and, yes, marry and eventually raise a family. Indeed, with each passing month as their relationship intensified, India felt her desire for *la vie bohème* slip stealthily away, surreptiously replaced by more quotidian ambitions. And she did not mind. Renzo was the one – the great love – for whom she would happily give up everything!

So it seemed to India as her little white '66 VW zipped down the Garden State Parkway, and she drew closer to the Keyport exit that today would bring her closer than ever to realizing this dream.

She pulled into the driveway of the tiny cottage and walked up the sandy path redolent with lilacs. Before she could ring the bell, Renzo opened the door and leaned over to kiss her on both cheeks – one of his many European mannerisms that charmed India.

"You look lovely, as always. I'll get my bag, and we'll go," Renzo said, leaving her standing in the foyer. Returning with a small duffle, he shepherded her toward his red Beetle and opened the passenger door for her. He had the top down, and as they pulled onto Route 36, the breeze whipped through her hair and drowned out their conversation.

So much for the careful coiffure her mother had helped her style. India smiled to herself behind her shades and put her head on Renzo's shoulder. She was content not to speak; just to be close to him was blissfully liberating. The majestic scenery of the Atlantic Highlands flashed by. They crossed the causeway toward Sandy Hook, and it wasn't long before Renzo let the Beetle skitter to a stop behind the tall dunes near the bath house.

"See you in a few minutes," he said as he headed to the men's changing rooms.

"It's going to take me bit longer to get this makeup off," India thought to herself. But when she did emerge some ten minutes later, having showered and peeled herself into her skimpy black bikini, there was no sign of Renzo. She shielded her eyes and scanned the beach, but there was no hint of him. The Beetle was where they had left it.

Hopping impatiently from one foot to another, India, who found any kind of waiting a torture, tried to quiet the litany of fears which automatically sprang to mind. After another five minutes had passed, an older gentleman left the men's locker room. India hesitated and then approached him.

Apologizing, she asked if he had seen her boyfriend in there.

"Yeah, I think there was a guy in the other stall."

"Was he OK?"

"Don't know, lady," he retorted, heading off toward the beach before India could importune him further.

India felt the familiar maelstrom of panic rise in her throat, and hot tears stung her eyes. As she was debating her next step, Renzo appeared, and India hastily turned away, wiped her eyes and forced a brave smile.

"Sorry, honey. You won't believe this but I couldn't figure this suit out." He gestured at the small pair of zebra-striped bathing trunks with a wraparound front panel that tied at the waist like a mini-sarong. "They're supposed to be the latest in Milano. I saw them in *L'Uomo* last month and ordered, but they are a devil to get into." He grinned ingenuously. "Do you like the suit?"

India nodded speechlessly. As a rule she liked everything about Renzo, but the bathing costume was a little over the top.

“You look terrific,” he said before she could recover. They walked down the beach and set up their blanket and umbrella as far away from other sunbathers as possible.

“Race you,” Renzo challenged and headed off into the surf. By the time India caught up and put her toes tentatively in the freezing brine, Renzo was out beyond the breakers swimming parallel to the rolling whitecaps. India slowly waded out up to her waist, grimacing each time the swells splashed her. She waved at Renzo who saw her heading back to the beach. Diving through a breaker, he stood up facing her and shook himself off like a shaggy puppy.

Bending down, he scooped her up into his arms and carried her out past the surf. She threw her arms around his neck and hung on for dear life. India did not swim particularly well, but she hesitated to show her terror. Instead, she pressed her cheek against Renzo’s and closed her eyes. She felt his soft and salty lips cover hers, and she gave in to the blissful sensation of floating in his arms.

Back on the blanket she smoothed coconut-scented oil onto his shoulder blades, letting her arms slip around his neck and down onto his firm, olive-toned chest, lightly tracing a path through the tufts of dark, curly hair. Renzo’s strong hands closed over her tiny ones and gave them a little squeeze, before he disengaged himself.

She sighed slightly and settled down next to him. They lay staring at the cloudless blue sky punctuated by arpeggios of soaring gulls. The heat lulled them into drowsiness and like a magnetic current drew their bodies closer. All at once, India felt Renzo turn onto his side and then lean over her and claim a lingering kiss. In the heat of the day and the blaze of her passion, she simply let herself go. It was Renzo who ultimately checked himself, planting a sweet peck on the top of her nose.

"It's late. We should get back. I made dinner reservations for us at Buona Sera. My brother Hugo and his wife are joining us."

Renzo was already packing up the blanket and umbrella so he did not have the time to notice the look of disappointment which had crossed India's face.

****

India adjusted the spaghetti straps of her slim orange linen sheath and surveyed herself in the full-length mirror. She piled her dark curls up on her head casually and fastened them with a barrette. She liked what she saw and hoped Renzo did, too. He had been chivalrous in insisting that she change in his bedroom while he used the small bathroom down the hall.

Before she stepped out, she couldn't resist peeking in Renzo's closet. There hung in perfect order a row of sleek, dark-colored suits all impeccably tailored in the European mode. Next to them were the requisite selection of long-sleeved shirts – mostly white cotton, but a few pastel silks as well. She ran her hands over the shoulders and down the lapels of one particularly fine navy jacket. The light worsted had a sensuous feel, and impetuously she wrapped the sleeves around her waist and leaned into the imaginary model. A knock on the door made her close the closet with guilty haste, grab her purse, and, donning a cheerful face, join the waiting Renzo.

Buona Sera was already crowded when she made her entrance on Renzo's arm. The maître d' took them directly to a prime table in a candlelit corner where Hugo and Maryann were sipping cocktails. Hugo, an older, grayer, stouter version of Renzo, stood up and greeted them warmly. A round of quick introductions was followed by Renzo's order of two champagne cocktails for India and himself, some brief chitchat, and then an escape into the menus.

"Let's have the lobster thermador," Renzo proposed to India. "It's the specialty." India looked a little hesitantly at the price, but she nodded in assent as Renzo whispered, "It's a celebration."

"Yes, indeed," Hugo chimed in. "Maryann and I have been so eager to meet you. My brother never stops talking about you."

"All good, I hope," India quipped, shifting a little nervously on her banquette.

"What else?" Hugo replied a little too loudly. "We Almansis have excellent taste in women."

India smiled awkwardly and lowered her eyes to her lap. She relaxed only when she felt Renzo's hand steal under the table and settle gently on her knee. Their eyes met, and she sucked in a breath of relief.

The dinner hour went better than she had expected. Hugo dominated the conversation, regaling India with stories about his five children, his construction business, his motorboat, and the pleasures of living at the Jersey Shore. Renzo seemed content to let his oldest sibling hold forth exuberantly, to savor his lobster and champagne, and to drape his arm affectionately around India's waist.

After tiramisù and brandies were served, the foursome got up to dance. It was a cha-cha which both India and Renzo attacked with an Arthur Murray diligence, but little real abandon. As the band segued into a slow fox trot, she smiled. "That's more like it!" As she settled into Renzo's arms, she felt a tap on her shoulder, and Hugo cut in on his brother.

"You don't mind, do you, brother? I want to dance with your pretty lady." India smiled wanly as Renzo obligingly switched partners. For all his bulk Hugo was a surprisingly athletic and engaging dancer. He gracefully maneuvered India away from Maryann and Renzo, and holding her at a tasteful arm's length, launched into the monologue he had been preparing all evening.

"Renzo is crazy about you, and I can see why. We were getting worried about him, you know?" India's eyes were quizzical, but she remained silent. "I mean he is already twenty-six and has not had a serious romance until now," Hugo rebounded. Still India remained mute. 'You're the perfect girl for him, and I can see that. You're Sicilian, and you're smart and beautiful." He flashed the contagious Almansi smile. "He'll have our family's blessing. My dad is already seventy, and he wants to see all his kids settled, you know, with great wives and houses and children. You want children, don't you?" he blurted out, suddenly holding India away from him.

India seemed stunned, but she managed to stammer, “Well, yes, of course, eventually. I’m still in college.”

“Yes, I know,” Hugo lowered his voice and pulled India closer so that he could launch the next salvo directly into her ear. “And that’s what I wanted to say to you. I know you’re brilliant. Renzo says so, and, of course, you’ll want to get that degree, but maybe you should consider taking a little break. You could always go back to it after you’re married – after you’ve had a baby or two.”

His eyes searched India’s, which flooded with confusion. “I’m just saying, honey, that I think Renzo is ready to propose, and knowing my brother, he won’t ask twice. You get my meaning?” he asked imperatively.

India simply nodded, dumbfounded. “It’s taken a long time for him to be ready to take the plunge,” Hugo whispered. “Don’t let this chance slip away – for both of you,” he added conspiratorially.

He escorted India back to the table where Maryann and Renzo also appeared to be sharing secrets. Without sitting, Hugo addressed his wife. “Let’s go, baby. It’s late, and I have to go visit a job site early tomorrow morning. We’ll leave these two lovebirds alone.”

Continental kisses were exchanged, and Renzo accompanied his brother and sister-in-law to the door where they paused for a minute. India watched them exchange a few private comments before Renzo turned back, stopping first at the bandstand to make a request. As he reached the table, the musicians had already struck up *Moon River*, and he swept India to her feet and waltzed her out to the dance floor. The lights were low; Hugo was gone, and India suddenly felt a surge of emotion. She melted into Renzo's arms and did not resist as he pressed his hips against hers and his lips onto her bare shoulders.

****

"A perfect evening," Renzo pronounced as he handed India a gold-rimmed porcelain cup of perfect espresso. They had returned to the house ostensibly for India to get her things. She sat on the sofa, and Renzo plopped down beside her. She kept her eyes focused intently on the dark roast and sipped slowly. She did not dare engage Renzo's glance, though she desperately wanted to. She knew if she did, he would read the storm of questions in hers. She felt him settle himself back on the cushions and drape his arm languidly across the back of the sofa. She checked the urge to lean back against his chest. That would be too forward; it was Renzo's move to make. And for what seemed an eternity as India stared into her empty cup, Renzo remained still and silent.

"I should go," she said without conviction and set down her cup. Before she could hoist herself to her feet, however, she felt Renzo's arms encircle her and push her back into the soft cushions. His lips hungrily found hers, then her forehead, then her eyes, her throat, and her cleavage. He paused and looked her deep in the eyes, searching for permission, for some answer perhaps. India closed hers and threw her head back, breathing deeply. As if this was the sign he awaited, Renzo's slender fingers gently slipped the spaghetti straps of her bodice down over her shoulders, and with a graceful arching of his body, covered India's with his.

How long their embraces lasted India could not later remember. It seemed they were two bodies suspended in space, two beings transported in time. So, when India suddenly heard Renzo's voice, sounding strangely choked, she was confused. Where was she? What was happening? Why was Renzo standing above her hastily buttoning his shirt and extending a hand to help her up.

"You should go," he said weakly. "It's either that or you'll have to sleep in the bathtub and lock the door," he said in an attempt to recover his poise.

India accepted his proffered hand and sat up slowly. She adjusted her dress and swept up her hair that had come cascading around her shoulders. Unsteadily, she rose to her feet, brushed past Renzo, and gathering her purse, headed blindly for the door. Renzo intercepted her and planted a conciliatory kiss on her forehead.

"Drive safely and call me when you get home. I'll wait up." She managed a nod.

Once in the car she gunned the engine and headed down the dirt beach road toward Route 36. By the time she reached the macadam, the tears had morphed into uncontrollable sobs.

What had gone wrong? Why didn't he see how much she loved him – how much she wanted him – how sure she was that it was OK. Even God would forgive them; they were in love, after all, and they would marry. They could marry now if that's what Renzo wanted. She didn't care what her parents would say. If Renzo wanted her, she would be his. Isn't that what Hugo had been trying to tell her?

"This is all my fault," she thought, and her sobs redoubled. She had been so cautious this whole year – the little Italian Catholic girl protecting her virginity, and then tonight she had startled him with her receptivity. It was only natural that, after a year of gentlemanly controlled passion, Renzo felt guilty for his advances. Oh, why couldn't she make him understand how much she loved him, how much she was ready to throw all those conventions to the wind – how <u>nothing</u> else mattered.

As the last words echoed in her ears and pounded behind her aching eyeballs, India swerved to the left and, rather than heading north, chose the Parkway South. It was only a few minutes before she realized her error. She had executed the cloverleaf and was pointed toward the Keyport/Leonardo exit. Feeling all her resistance and self-control melt away, she slowed through the tolls and pulled over to the bank of phone booths on the right. She stumbled out of the car and automatically dialed Renzo's number.

"Sweetheart, you can't be home already," he answered on the first ring. "Are you OK?" he bleated into the phone, and as she dissolved into loud sobs, he did not even wait for an affirmative. "Where are you?" he shouted, and waiting only for a single exit number, blurted out, "Stay there. I'll come get you."

****

Still weeping, India had slumped over the wheel of her car when Renzo's Beetle flashed his lights and pulled into the space beside hers. She squinted into the headlights and wiped her red, swollen eyes. Unsteadily, she got out of the front seat and threw herself on Renzo's neck, burying her face on his shoulder. Without a word, he removed his jacket and placed it around her shoulders and started to lead her back to her car. He seemed strangely quiet. India balked and stood still in her tracks; her terror stricken eyes implored him.

"Come on," he said, taking her by the elbow and opening the driver's door for her.

"What are we doing?" she moaned.

"I called your mother. You're going to follow me to your house," he said firmly.

"No!" she protested, "I can't drive. It's too late. Let me come back with you."

"If you do, you know what will happen," Renzo said in a resigned monotone.

"I can sleep in the tub –" She raised her voice hysterically.

"No, you can't."

"Really, I can if that's what you want. I don't mind. I just don't want to go home. Not tonight . . "

Renzo wheeled around and placed his hands on her shoulders. He lifted her chin until their eyes met, and he said calmly, “We can’t, India.”

Renzo drove cautiously through the rain, constantly checking his rearview mirror for India’s car. The Parkway exits flashed by, but India did not count them. She abandoned herself to following Renzo with a numb resolve. “Best not to think – just drive – just get home,” she told herself. “We’ll fix everything tomorrow.”

Every light in the tiny Tudor house was ablaze as the two cars pulled into the driveway. Antoinette flung open the front door usually reserved only for company and, with exaggerated relief, welcomed in the prodigal pair. Despite the fact that it was now 1:30 in the morning, the parlor coffee table was set with coffee service and biscotti, white linen napkins and the matriarchal silver, as if Antoinette was accustomed to receiving “gentlemen callers” at this hour. Her insistent look told Renzo not to refuse. He sat tentatively on the edge of the blue damask sofa. India collapsed beside him, suddenly mortified.

“Please eat something, Renzo, and I’ll go fix up the spare room for you. You can leave after breakfast,” Antoinette offered in a tone that was really a command.

"No, Mrs. Bertolini, thanks. I can't. My family is expecting me early tomorrow morning. I just wanted to make sure India got home safely. It was my fault she was late."

Antoinette nodded and withdrew. "I'll leave you two to your coffee then."

India simply hung her head. Renzo waited until the dowager dragon was gone and then stood up.

"I'm going now, India," he said gently.

India rose and walked him into the foyer. She tilted her head expectantly. He hesitated a second and then planted a tender kiss on her cheek. The door closed behind him before she could utter another word.

India never saw him again – not until that autumn night a lifetime later.

# SAVED

"*Malpensa.*" Renata smiled wryly as the pilot repeated his announcement: "*Signore e Signori, incomminciamo a scendere a Milano. Noi arriveremo a Malpensa in quindici minuti.*" "What a crazy name for an airport! So Italian! All that drama. No bad thoughts today, though, " Renata thought. No, today was the beginning of her great European adventure – her first trip on her own away from home, away from her parents – her first chance to see all the places she had read about for the last twenty years!

The land of Dante and Petrarch, of Michelangelo and Raphael, of all the masters who had fired her imagination and filled her soul: the romantic land of her ancestors, the *paese* of sun and song and poetry! It was to be all hers that summer. She had earned it: a complete scholarship for summer study in Florence to perfect the language, read the *Divine Comedy*, drink in the art, paint a little. Her mother had not been able to refuse her. "It was an honor," her kindly advisor, Mr. Katz, had told Rosalie Alfieri. Sarah Lawrence so rarely awarded girls a complete ride, but he had known that Renata needed the grant if she was to go at all, and he had worked hard to convince the Dean on her behalf.

Rosalie had moaned and worried and invented a myriad of ailments and excuses for why Renata should not go alone, but in the end she had been defeated by her daughter's dogged perseverance. She had resigned herself to letting her "baby" out of sight for a whole six weeks and had morosely packed Renata's suitcases with every imaginable precautionary remedy – homemade medicines, vitamins, rosary beads, scapula, St. Christopher's medal – practical and metaphysical talismen to ward off the terrible unforeseen to be wrought by separation.

Renata had not slept a wink on the long night flight from JFK, but she was wide awake as the Alitalia jet swooped over the looming Alps and touched down with a shuddery lurch.

It was midmorning by the time the taxi delivered Renata to her modest *pensione* on Via Giuseppi Mazzini. Her Italian was serviceable enough to pay the cabby and exchange pleasantries with the bellman who ushered her into a tiny single room on the backside of the hotel. It was furnished with a single bed, a wooden chair, and a truncated excuse for a desk. A solitary bare light bulb dangled from the ceiling. The bellman deposited her bulging suitcase on the bed and with a flourish drew back the graying lace curtains and raised the window halfway. A brick wall stood a few feet away blocking the already oppressive mid-morning sun.

"Not exactly a room with a view!" Renata sighed as the bellman took his leave. But she wouldn't be spending much time indoors anyway. She had only three days in Milan before she was to catch the train and join her Sarah Lawrence classmates in Florence.

Showered and changed, camera around her neck, Renata emerged from her dismal cell and walked briskly toward the piazza. The filigree ramparts of the Duomo rose majestically above the city beckoning her. Within minutes she was standing in the square before the great cathedral's central portal. Looking up at the riot of gingerbread carvings – spires and flying buttresses, gargoyles and saints – made her dizzy.

This towering cathedral suddenly took on a kinetic presence. It seemed as if the stone façade were advancing toward her, the great doors a gaping maw ready to swallow her up. Shrunk by some invisible, crushing force, she could only turn and run or enter into the abyss. Her heart pounding and her breath hiccupping in choppy gasps, Renata hastened through the portal into the nave.

The cool darkness was soothing, and the prismic kaleidoscope of color from the stained glass was hypnotizing. She wandered aimlessly through the aisles, robotically attaching herself to an English-speaking tour group. Before she knew it, she found herself in an elevator with half a dozen British tourists ascending to the bulwark.

When Renata stepped out onto the narrow walkway above the city, her knees almost buckled. She fell to the back of the group, gripping the handrail and advancing tentatively until she could go no farther. As the Brits and their guide rounded a turn and disappeared from view, Renata sank to her haunches and collapsed against one of the granite pillars. Her head fell to her knees, and she fought desperately to breathe. Above her crumpled form hovered a huge grotesque, his wings spread like a menacing guardian. If she did not collect herself, he would seize her in his talons and hurl her from the parapet.

In a rush of panic, Renata scrambled to her feet and pressed her body against the inner wall, slithering toward the exit. She did not wait for the elevator, but clattered down the spiral stone steps to the nave and fled into the piazza.

The square, which a short time before had been bathed in sunlight, now stood drenched by a sudden summer cloudburst. Pedestrians had opened their umbrellas and were scurrying toward the Galleria to escape the downpour.

Swept along by the human throng, Renata followed, a rudderless bark in search of any port. The raindrops danced before her eyes; they blinded her, refracting the light from the mirrored panels and glass ceiling of the opulent Galleria Vittorio Emanuele. She fled through the glass-covered arcade, fighting her way back into the busy street.

Faces loomed before her – horrible, swollen, contorted faces that blocked her path and shrieked after her. Rain filled her nostrils and tumbled down her cheeks together with the torrent of her tears. Stumbling through the narrow streets, Renata propelled herself toward the *pensione*, where, after fumbling with the room lock, she felt the door open. She crawled into her dark cave, threw herself on the bed, and reached for the telephone.

****

Renata's hand tried to grasp the receiver, but it eluded her. Her body was floating above the bed, swirling down into a spiraling vortex in whose depths a grotesque stone edifice with granite tendrils reached out to clutch her. Above, the menacing gargoyles spread their wings, rendering the darkness complete. From the black hell of this ninth circle, chimes sounded like a knell. Renata stretched her hand out and this time connected with the pealing instrument. Before she could lift it from its cradle, she opened her eyes and slowly took in her surroundings.

In the small bedroom with blue cornflower wallpaper, the phone had stopped ringing. With great effort she sat up in bed and pushed her bangs back from her sweaty forehead. The sun was pouring in through the two small windows. "It was already late morning," Renata thought. "Why had she slept so long?"

Outside the closed door she heard Rosalie sign off softly, "Yes, I'll tell her you called. She's still asleep." And before Renata could call out to contradict her mother, she heard the receiver click and the roar of the vacuum cleaner, banging aggressively into the walls of the corridor outside her room.

"I'm awake, Mother!" Renata yelled, but the din drowned her words. She propped up her pillows and sank back against them with resignation. Somehow she didn't have the strength to argue. Not today but perhaps tomorrow she would have to do something; she had to escape this prison. She had to make her way back to her old life. But how? Where?

Her mind was a complete haze; she glanced at the book lying open on the nightstand - Elizabeth Barrett Browning; she must have been reading poetry last night. Next to the white-and-gold-bound volume stood a vase of roses. "That wasn't there last night," Renata struggled to recall. Fumbling for a card, she almost knocked over the glass of water and bottle of pills. To her dismay there was none. Rosalie must have removed it. She would have to quiz her mother. No doubt it was from a friend of whom Rosalie disapproved.

"Not Anthony, alas," Renata sighed. She hadn't heard from him in over a year. It was truly over. At first that had been hard to believe. They had been so deeply in love, or so it seemed to Renata. For two years they had gone everywhere together. And though they had never spoken of marriage, Renata had simply assumed it would follow her graduation.

"Fool that I am!" she muttered bitterly to herself, "to believe in fairy tales." But she had not been alone in that belief. Her father and her mother, the normally vigilant and possessive Rosalie, had endorsed the match and turned a blind eye when Anthony and her daughter spent hours alone at his beach house. Anthony's own sister had welcomed Renata to their family, conspiratorially arranging romantic rendezvous for her brother and his girl. The script seemed to have a predictable ending, and then, inexplicably, Anthony had turned their world on end. He had showed up one Saturday night for their date and instead of taking her to the opera or Sardi's, he had driven to a quiet overlook atop the Palisades.

Breathlessly, Renata anticipated a seduction, and in her heart she knew she would not resist. Instead, Anthony turned off the engine, faced her slowly in the front seat and, taking her hand, gently said, "Renata, we can't go on like this. It's not fair to you. You deserve someone who will love you forever and give you a family. I'm not that guy. I'll never have kids or a wife for that matter. Do you understand what I am telling you?"

Renata did not – not at that terrible moment – not until some months later when a New York friend told her she had seen Anthony with a man in a Greenwich Village bar.

By the time the realization had sunk in, Renata felt herself at a loss to comprehend it in any meaningful way. She raced through her junior year at Sarah Lawrence, intent only on finishing school and getting away. She threw herself into existence with a crazed passion, and in every waking hour she had found some activity to absorb her energy, to help her to forget. She volunteered for Robert Kennedy; she canvassed for low-cost housing; she marched for civil rights, and as the war accelerated, she found the local Peace Center and fell in with friends whose ideals she shared: friends Rosalie did not approve of – friends like Gabriel.

"Did Gabe send the flowers, Mother?" Renata questioned sharply as Rosalie unceremoniously pushed open the bedroom door and entered with a breakfast tray.

"Ah, you are finally up!" Rosalie said tartly. Brushing aside the very flowers about which she had been queried without an answer, she set the oatmeal, juice, and coffee on the nightstand.

"Actually, I've been awake for a while. How could I help it when you're vacuuming outside the door. And the telephone? Who was it on the phone?"

"Nothing important, sweetie."

"Was it Gabe?" Renata persisted.

"I told him you hadn't slept well and needed to rest. He said he'd call back."

"I was awake. I wanted to speak to him. He sent the flowers, didn't he?"

"Yes, I suppose he did. So what?" Rosalie countered with belligerence.

"I want to thank him – for caring, for keeping my spirits up this summer. I'd be going crazy here if he didn't come to visit."

"And whose fault is that?" Rosalie seethed.

"What's that supposed to mean? Do you think I purposely had this meltdown? Do you think I purposely screwed up in Italy?"

"No, dear," Rosalie said, trying to sound contrite. "You're ill. You can't help it. Your nerves are shot because you are rundown. You were coming down with mono before you left for Milan. I shouldn't have let you go – "

"No, Mother! I was not! I don't have mono now, and you know it!"

"Dr. Susskind says the blood tests are not conclusive."

"Nonsense, Mother. You can tell your church friends that story if you want, but don't expect me to believe it or tell my friends lies."

"What friends?" Rosalie rejoined bitterly. "Gabe?"

"Yes, Gabe, Lisa, my real friends," Renata sputtered, choking back the rising emotion. "Friends who accept me for who I am – who don't expect me to be perfect."

"I never asked for perfection, sweetie," Rosalie tried cajoling. "Here, eat before it gets cold."

Renata reluctantly took a mouthful and swallowed with difficulty. "I'm not perfect, Mother. In fact, I'm pretty far from it, and you and I are going to have to live with that. If there's anything these two months of seeing a shrink have taught me, it's to be realistic about my expectations. I wasn't ready to go to Europe on my own. I should have known that."

"And you would have been fine if you hadn't gotten sick."

"I did not get sick!" Renata screamed. "I had a major panic attack – a mental crisis. And do you know why? Because I was completely adrift. I had never, not once in twenty years, ever been alone – on my own without your being there. I was terrified – disoriented – hallucinating – " She broke off and pushed the food tray away.

Rosalie gently removed it and sat on the bed. "Sh-sh, sweetie. I know you're upset. It's been a rough year, getting sick - " Renata's eyes flashed daggers, and Rosalie hurried on, "breaking up with Anthony, too. I know what he meant to you, how much you loved him. We all loved him – your father and I, too. He would have been a perfect husband for you."

"No, Mother, he wouldn't have! I've told you."

Rosalie cut her off. "Who knows? Perhaps he'll come to his senses."

"He won't. He can't. I've told you – "

"Ah, sweetie, I don't believe all that talk. He was so generous to you. He'd have been a good provider – not like your father."

"Let's not go there, Mother."

"I'm just saying he had so many strong points – handsome, smart, cultured –"

"Italian and Catholic – let's not forget those! Oh, yes, and gay, Mother. Gay – a little obstacle to happily ever after."

"Stop speaking nonsense, Renata," Rosalie rose angrily. "You are hysterical. You haven't taken your morning wellbutrin." She reached for the pills and offered them to Renata with the orange juice. She was not prepared for the backward sweep of her daughter's hand which knocked the pills to the floor and spilled the juice all over the Wedgewood chintz spread.

"Get out! Leave me alone!" Renata shouted. "I am sick to death of doctors and their pills and you and your excuses. Stop apologizing for me. Stop being sorry I am who I am!"

Renata had risen to her feet and advanced toward Rosalie, who was backing away shakily juggling the breakfast board. Pale, but still formidable, Rosalie recovered herself for an instant, and, framed in the doorway, she spit out, "I love who you are."

"Do you?" Renata snarled. "You should. You've made me the way I am."

She slammed the door on the retreating Rosalie with exaggerated force, swung around, and, steadying her shoulders against the wooden panels, slid down to the ground. Hugging her knees, she let her head drop and shook with sobs. Only when the spasms had subsided and the sounds outside the door were stilled did Renata raise herself up and walk to the bed stand. Lifting the phone, she dialed Gabe's number.

****

Wearing a fashionable kaftan with her hair piled up on her head, Renata looked remarkably composed, though her eyes were still red as she settled herself at the edge of her bed. Opposite her sat Gabriel Sorensen. He had come the instant she had called him, and as he now perched on the uncomfortable wooden desk chair, he apologized for his attire.

"I'm sorry. I was working on the Triumph when you called. You sounded urgent so I didn't bother to change," he grinned, running his fingers through his tousled blond hair.

Renata smiled wanly. "Thanks." She noticed for the first time how ingratiating Gabe's smile was. His lips, thin and bow-shaped, arched into a lopsided crinkle, his dimples dancing in his cheeks. "How did you manage to get past the dragon?" Renata asked.

"She didn't look too pleased, but she let me in."

"Be grateful she wasn't glad to see you or she'd be sitting here with us, serving tea! At least we're alone."

"So what happened?" Gabe asked gently, leaning forward, his hands clasped over his knees.

"We had a big blowout over Anthony and Milan and . . ." Renata interrupted herself. She stared hard at Gabriel's face, so full of caring. There was openness and honesty in his features. His blue eyes radiated acceptance; his square-cut jaw seemed determined yet gentle and supportive. "That's it – supportive," she thought. Gabe took her for who she was, and he seemed to like that person.

They had met at a peace rally. Renata was manning a table with anti-draft literature, and Gabe was passing out flyers encouraging young men to sign conscientious objector declarations. After a brief, sympathetic exchange between them, Gabe had moved away into the crowd and, moments later, was arrested for not having a permit. The police had ordered Renata to pack up her table, too, and it wasn't until several days later that she learned from the head of her organization, Mervin, that Gabe had been released on his own recognizance. He showed up a few days afterwards at the Peace Center where Renata volunteered, ostensibly to pick up some more literature. This time their eyes locked for a very long while.

After that they shared an occasional coffee when the two were working at the Center, though Renata, on the rebound from Anthony and planning a summer abroad, had hinted to Gabe that she didn't want any involvements at this point in her life. She had confided to him about how Anthony had broken her heart, how all her plans for marriage and children and domestic bliss had fallen apart and how she felt rudderless and alone. He had said nothing, simply smiled that same quiet smile he was now giving her.

Without a word, Gabe reached into his knapsack and handed Renata a clumsily wrapped package. "Maybe this will make you feel better," he said sweetly.

Renata took the parcel and opened it speedily. She loved presents! "Oh, Gabe, this is wonderful!" she exclaimed as she discovered it contained Kahlil Gibran's *The Prophet*.

"Look inside. I wrote something for you."

Renata's fingers trembled as she found the flyleaf. There in Gabe's unmistakable, awkward scrawl was the terse inscription: *Love is our pursuit of wholeness for our desire to be complete. The union of two souls is life's highest bliss.*

"That's beautiful, Gabe. I didn't know you liked poetry."

"Yeah, I do – didn't get to read much of it when I was an engineering student, but I hope to make up for that now," he replied shyly.

"What are your plans, Gabe?" Renata asked.

"To beat the draft and then go back to school – to study something I love to do – to do something with my life that really matters," he answered without hesitation. "And you?"

"Finish school, too, and then get out of here – get a job – go to Paris maybe – that is, if I can learn to live on my own. I made such a mess of it this time," she faltered, lowering her eyes to her lap to hide the emotion.

"No, you didn't. It just wasn't the right time. But if you leave this time, it doesn't have to be alone."

His words pierced Renata's heart. She raised her glance to meet his and held it steady. He saw the pleading in her eyes, and so he continued.

"I've known it since I first met you, Renata. Nothing else in my life has ever seemed so certain, so right. I have never been as sure of anything as I have been of my love for you." His words began to tumble out with unleashed abandon. "I know this is fast. I know it sounds crazy, but, Renata, I am even crazier for you."

"I know," she whispered.

"I know what you are thinking. You are thinking about Anthony." She shook her head. "And about your parents? I'm thinking about mine, too, but we won't be like they are. We won't make the same mistakes. We won't stay together just because of the kids. We'll be together because we have to – we want to – because there is no other way! I hate being alone, too. I don't know what this war is going to bring, but if we face it together, there's nothing we can't do. We'll be OK. We'll have each other."

Renata reached out her hand and clasped his. "I won't let anything happen to you, and we will never be apart. We'll take care of each other, no natter what happens."

Gabriel replied with his signature smile before he leaned over and planted a deep kiss on her parted lips. "Is that a 'yes'?" Renata nodded and broke into a tearful smile.

"Renata?" She heard the sharp tones from the hallway. Had Rosalie been listening at the door? "Her timing is ridiculously annoying," Renata observed.

Gabriel stood up. "I guess I better be going. We can deal with them tomorrow."

Renata stood, too, reached to her nightstand and picked up the copy of *Sonnets to the Portuguese.* "I have nothing to give you in return," she said, indicating the Gibran volume, "except this."

He pressed the book to his heart and took her in his arms one more time before turning to go. His hand was on the doorknob when Renata spoke, "Read it tonight and tell me what you think."

He paused without looking back. "What's your favorite?" he asked softly.

"*Go from me/Yet I feel I shall stand/Henceforth in thy shadow. Nevermore/ Alone upon the threshold of my door of individual life, I shall command/ The uses of my soul - "*

Gabe's voice chimed in: *"The widest land/ Doom takes to part us, leaves thy heart in mine/ With pulses that beat double."* He turned back in time to catch a look of joyful surprise illuminate Renata's face.

"You know it then?"

"Uh, hmm,"

“Robert saved Elizabeth,” Renata murmured.

“They saved each other.” And again flashing his crooked grin, he was gone.

# ABSCHIED

"What am I doing here?" she asked aloud as she hoisted her overnight bag up onto the bed. The surroundings were familiar enough – the plush wing chair at the fireplace, the floral chintz bedspread and drapes, the English hunt scenes adorning the walls and the view from the window across the tall white portico and onto Freeport's busy Main Street.

No, it was not the stately old Harraseeket Inn itself which felt strange to Maya. It was the eerie singleness of the room – the odd absence of someone to share the getaway – not just anyone – but Marius – Marius Martin, her husband, lover, soul mate, friend who should have been with her now of all days, their forty-first wedding anniversary.

But Marius was gone – the life cruelly snatched from him some months before as he exercised on the treadmill – *a sudden tightening*, as her poet cousin had described it at the memorial service. And so today when Maya and Marius would surely have been celebrating together somewhere special – Acadia perhaps – she was alone.

Well, not entirely alone, Maya conceded as she headed out to her car. She had brought Barbary and Starbuck with her for companionship and comfort. She lifted the cat carrier from the back seat, snapped the leash on the big, black bear dog, and walked back to the hotel.

When she had told her local friends her plan for the day, they had raised their eyebrows quizzically. "Are you sure?" one neighbor had asked. "Won't there be too many memories?"

"I want to remember," Maya had insisted. "I want to spend time with Marius. We never said goodbye."

Once inside the hotel, the Newfoundland began busily sniffing around the room, as Maya set up a cat tent with Starbuck's bed, toys, and dishes. How many times had Marius and she gone through the same ritual in hotel rooms along the East Coast, while they were showing the venerable Maine Coon to Supreme Grand Champion status. The still regal "Boo," as they nicknamed him, was not a stranger to hotels or travel. He relished the attention, the treats, the luxury. He always sought out the most comfortable spot in a room. She and Marius would joke that Starbuck would rate hotel rooms with discrimination – only five-paw accommodations such as the Harraseeket met his approval. He had been here ten years before when he had competed in the big Cat Fanciers Association show at the Portland Civic Center. As he now pranced cautiously around the room, his whiskers alert, his lynx-tipped ears pricked, he seemed to be remembering.

Only Barbary had no previous connection to the place. He had entered Maya's life on an impulse after Marius' death. He was still a big, galumphing puppy who knew only Maya without Marius – or did he? Sometimes Maya thought Barbary sensed a presence in the house or on the beach or in the woods, and then the dog would stand erect and give a tiny moan, his brown eyes staring into the unseen. "Ah, those eyes," Maya sighed as she patted the dog's head. "Look into his eyes, and you will see me," the medium had told her channeling Marius' voice. Maya gave a little shudder and returned to her unpacking.

She put her lingerie in the drawer and set out the black sheath dress on the bed. Silly to dress up for dinner alone in Maine, but the dress was another connection to Marius. She had worn it to their fortieth anniversary dinner in Bar Harbor last fall – such a joyous celebration! They had sipped champagne in their room overlooking Frenchman's Bay. They had watched the cruise ships' lights flicker through the slate blue haze before adjourning to the restaurant for a delectable meal. Then they had finished with a nightcap in the Blue Nose's lounge where Marius had requested the piano player to serenade his wife with Cole Porter's *So in Love.*

Maya felt the lump rise in her throat and the tears sting sharply as she involuntarily hummed the tune:

*Strange dear but true dear*
*When I'm close to you dear –*
*The stars fill the sky*
*So in love with you am I.*

She stopped herself from singing but not before whispering one of the last lines: *I'm yours till I die.*

Turning abruptly, she reached for Barbary's leash. "Let's go, sweet pea. You need a walk." She scooped up Starbuck and put him in his tent for safekeeping. "We won't be long, Boo Boo." The cat merely yawned.

Barbary waved his plumed tail and led the way. Heads popped up over newspapers as they crossed the elegant lobby. Maya loved the stir Barbary always created; it often helped break the ice for conversation with strangers now that her days were filled with silence. They ambled down one side of Main Street and back up the other. Pausing to peek into the hotel gift shop, Maya spied a ridiculously expensive, handsome catnip mat. For Starbuck, she decided, as she paid the cashier, who kindly threw a dog biscuit into the bag as well.

The magnificent old cat was fourteen now – on borrowed time for the breed. His gait was rickety; his coat had thinned; his muscle tone had begun to atrophy, and yet he retained the look – the proud, flashing green gold eyes and the square cut muzzle thrust forward jauntily. Returning to the room, Maya silenced the progression of this train of thought.

"I'm going to take a swim, guys," she said aloud – a habit of rhetorically addressing her pets that had only intensified in the long, quiet months following Marius' death. "Perhaps another sign of my going crazy," she wondered, but, in point of fact, she didn't really care. "Barbary, you babysit Starbuck," she commanded.

The solarium was deserted. "Just as well," thought Maya. The late afternoon sun streaming through the glass was hypnotic. She waded into the heated turquoise water and swam a few laps, then turned on her back and just floated. Her eyes closed, she felt herself buoyed up by an unseen pair of arms – Marius', as he had so often supported her when they swam together. The water rocked her gently into a meditative lull.

Her random thoughts meandered back to an article she had read that morning in *The Newf Tide* about Rigel, the Newfoundland hero of the Titanic, who had swum in the freezing North Atlantic waters for three hours, first searching for his drowned master, and then circling a lifeboat while barking for help until the rescue ship *Carpathian* arrived. "Amazing creatures!" she thought, flipping over and swimming to the ladder. She was glad she had not come to the Harraseeket alone after all.

****

Dinner passed more quickly and pleasantly than she had imagined it would. The innkeeper, a spirited octogenarian, was making hostess rounds, and when she discovered that it had been Maya and Marius' anniversary custom to dine here, she promptly sat down and had sent over a round of complimentary cocktails. The two women found they had a surprising number of things in common, and drinks had segued into dinner. It was late when Maya found herself thanking the woman profusely for her kindness and hurrying off to her room.

After a quick walk with Barbary and changing into her nightdress, Maya liberated Starbuck from his tent and placed the brand new catnip mat on the other pillow of the king-sized bed. Magnetically drawn, Starbuck pounced onto the bed and with a flourish settled himself on the mat. Not to be outdone, Barbary hauled himself up and plopped his huge frame down across the folded quilt at the foot of the bed.

Despite the double martini, Maya didn't yet feel sleepy, so she reached for the remote and flipped through channels. *Great Performances* was airing a concert from the Vienna Philharmonic, and there she stopped her search. Muti had just taken the podium with baritone Thomas Hampson. The breathtaking silence was followed by the haunting melancholy strains of Mahler. Maya closed her eyes and settled against the pillows as the last movement of *Das Lied von der Erde* washed over her. *Der Abschied – the farewell- Letzten Lebewohl – I want to bid him a last farewell.*

Tears began to fall silently down her cheeks as Starbuck's rhythmic purring harmonized with the singer's sorrow: *You leave me long alone!* Absently, her hand reached out to caress the frail, bony frame. How soon before Starbuck, too, would be gone? This evening, this crazy evening at the hotel was just one more goodbye. Or perhaps it was not a new parting but only the same long, leave-taking, a continuum of the one she never had gotten to utter to Marius – an opportunity to rewrite the last act, to erase regret, to say all the things that should be said before the abyss engulfed her, too.

She bent down and planted a kiss on the old cat's head, and, nonplussed, Starbuck yawned and languidly stretched out a paw – a sovereign demanding homage. Barbary, sensing Maya's need, lumbered up to lick her face before inserting himself between his mistress and the cat. Starbuck leaned into the warm, luxurious fur and curled himself contentedly against Barbary's chest. With a sigh, Maya let herself collapse into the heap of snoring, purring fur and clung to the contented creatures as if they were a life raft. This was her rescue! Like Rigel, Barbary was plucking her from the surging torrents of grief.

*Ewig – forever – ewig.* The singer's fading lament seemed to link together the goodbyes of the past with the imminent ones ahead. For Maya, time was a tortuous thread. But for Starbuck and Barbary, there was no thought of eternity – only the blessedness of this moment.

# THE ASSISTANT

It was already sweltering at 8:00 in the morning as Clemence Marguy stepped off the ferry and raced down the dock to hail a cab. Another August day in the city. She was glad she would be indoors in Derek's plush suite for most of the day. She checked her watch again as the cab drew up in front of the Essex House on Central Park South.

The doorman greeted her with a smile. Derek usually stayed here when he was at the Met, so they knew her. She darted by the front desk, stopped at the concierge for Derek's mail and took the elevator to the penthouse. Knowing Derek would still be asleep after last night's *Werther*, she quietly slipped her key into the lock and tiptoed into the apartment. She moved noiselessly down the hall past the singer's closed bedroom door and into the small front parlor he used as an office when he was on the road.

The desk was piled high with papers, books, sheet music, CDs, and faxes. Hadn't she tidied that all yesterday before she left? How in heaven's name could he make such a mess in so short a time? When the Baroness wasn't with him, Derek was even less organized than usual – if that were possible. "But think on the bright side," she counseled herself. "At least you don't have to put up with that woman's ordering you around as if you were her secretary, not her lover's assistant. And besides, that's why he needs me," she reassured herself, attacking the chaos.

By the time Clemence had checked her watch again, it was 11:00 a.m. She wished Derek would rouse himself; there was so much work they needed to accomplish together on this, one of his rare days off. He had somehow managed to sleep through three phone calls – probably had disconnected the extension in his room – and though the demands and deadlines were looming, Clemence knew better than to try to wake her sleeping boss. The one time she had, at the request of a frantic opera house manager who was panicking at the half-hour call for her delayed star, Derek had almost taken her head off.

No, Clemence knew it was better to let Derek make his own mistakes and then clean up after him. So far this morning she had promised the *Opera News* journalist, who had called for the third time, she would definitely get Derek Howe to commit later today to an interview time and call her back.

She had gone over the recital tour bookings with David, his manager at CAMI, and she had promised Aubrey Heath, his patient accompanist who was waiting for the call to rehearse, that she would call him the instant Derek emerged. "I'll need an hour first because we absolutely have to go over the Carnegie Hall program notes. They are due at 4:00 o'clock today, and he hasn't looked at them," she apologized.

Aubrey sighed, "Not your fault, darlin'. I've got my cell. I'm going to do errands. Call me, luv."

"I will call; I promise," she soothed.

"Call whom?" a deep melodic voice queried. Leaning against the doorframe, his longish dirty blond hair tousled, a morning shadow making his chiseled features all the more handsome, Derek Howe finally greeted the day.

"Well, actually, a whole list of people," Clemence replied brightly as Derek turned on his heel and headed to the kitchen.

"Coffee's made," she called after him, "and I need you for a couple of urgent things right away - if possible," she added, softening her approach. Clemence gathered up the folders, a pad and pen and seated herself in the wing chair awaiting Derek's attention.

The tenor padded back into the living room and plopped himself opposite her on the sofa. "Shoot," he grinned. "Any reviews yet from last night?"

"No, you know the *Times* won't be out until tomorrow morning, and the *Post* later today." Clemence made a mental note to intercept the papers. Derek hated critics, and he could not endure the slightest negative remark without obsessing and ranting, but somehow perversely, he always read them - that is unless Clemence got to the papers first. Missing pages was a trick the Baroness had taught her. "Shrewd," she mused.

Clemence was going methodically through her checklist with Derek when the phone rang again. This time Derek jumped up to get it. "Hello. Ah, *allo*," he purred. He stood up and signaled Clemence that he would take the call in the bedroom. "I got it," he yelled from down the hall. "Hang up, Clemence."

Clemence did, but not before she caught a crisp female voice say, "I'm in town for just twenty-four hours. Can we meet?" It was not the Baroness.

Five minutes later Derek reemerged from the bedroom smiling broadly. "I'm going to take a quick shower and then we'll go over the program. Block me out from 4:00 o'clock this afternoon until tomorrow morning. No calls, nothing. OK? Call the desk for a 'Do not disturb' – even Chérie."

Chérie was, of course, the Baroness. "That'll be a tough one," Clemence thought, as nothing stopped her when she was steamrolling, though perhaps in this case the time difference from Paris would work for Derek.

It was more than a half hour before Derek, smartly attired in gray slacks and a blue polo that matched his eyes, rejoined Clemence. "What you got?" he yawned.

"Aubrey will be here at 2:00 p.m. to rehearse. We need to go over the Carnegie Hall program, and then I'll walk it over there."

He fumbled through a pile of papers on the coffee table and pulled out a folder with the program notes. Rifling through them, he handed Clemence a stack with his scrawled pencil notations in the margins.

"The notes are great. You tie the Schumann and Whitman together brilliantly. Just add my name to the byline because we did do this together after all." He grinned his best boyish smile.

Clemence raised an eyebrow and checked her inclination to reply tartly. What had Derek actually done except read them to make sure he concurred?

Feeling her silence, Derek added, "You put my ideas into words so beautifully." And before Clemence could answer, he fired off another salvo: "Oh, and the translations – I caught a few errors in the German texts, and I'm not comfortable with your putting your name on them as translator. I mean, what does that mean really? You just supplied the English – "

"That's precisely what it means!" Clemence snapped, removing her eyeglasses and pretending to stare pointedly at him, when, in fact, without her glasses she couldn't see his expression at all.

"Well, it's just part of your job with the program. It's not that this is a literary work," Derek argued.

Clemence knew this discussion was going nowhere, but for some reason, she couldn't let it go today. "OK, if you don't want to use mine, we can use EMI's CD liner translations for the *Dichterliebe*, but then, of course, you'll have to pay royalties for that. Mine are free," she finished, an edge of sarcasm creeping into her voice. "Damn it, he should be paying me for the notes and translations and all the extra things I do," she thought bitterly. "Matt is right about that."

Sensing a tempest brewing, Derek sidestepped the whole issue. "Well, never mind. This time use our joint byline for both the texts and the notes. That should take care of it for now," he equivocated.

Clemence did not see how this solved anything. "Fine," she conceded wearily. "I'll make the changes and drop them off and head home a little early since you won't need me after 4:00 o'clock," she added curtly. "What time will you want to work tomorrow?" she asked, sounding more accusatory than she meant to be.

"Oh, I don't know. Don't call me. I'll call you when I get up."

Clemence knew what that meant – a morning of waiting at home for the summons, fielding calls from everyone Derek had shut out. She felt rather close to a primal scream but controlled herself. Turning her back to Derek, she sat down and called up the word files on the computer. Glad to be off the hook, Derek wandered back into the kitchen with as much nonchalance as he could muster.

****

Matt was surprised to find Clemence home with the dinner table set when he got in at 6:00 p.m. "You're early. Did His Highness fire you?" he asked her, only half joking.

"Not funny, Matt. No, he's incommunicado till tomorrow."

"Again?" Matt snorted. "Wonder who it is?"

"I have a good guess, but who cares. It's his business." Clemence found herself getting defensive even though she really didn't feel Derek deserved as much.

"I don't care about his personal life. I care about the way he takes you for granted. When are you going to stand up to him?" Matt demanded.

Her husband was right, but his tone rankled Clemence. It hinted of a kind of corporate superiority: Matt, the hugely successful investment manager presiding at home the way he did at the office. She had no intention of fueling his criticism by telling him about the translations. But somehow as they moved around the kitchen preparing dinner, the story came sailing out. And with each glass of cabernet that Matt poured, Clemence found her frustration with Derek redirected at her husband.

By the time dinner was over, Matt had taken her to task for working exclusively for Derek, for not taking on other clients and moving on to work for David in a managerial capacity. That Clemence had gotten to participate in so many exciting, creative projects with Derek – "without giving you your share of the credit," Matt had countered – that she and sometimes Matt, too, had traveled all over the States and Europe attending openings and festivals with Derek's glamorous inner circle – no comment from Matt – that Derek had promised her a raise this year and they had two amazing television projects planned –

"Promises," Matt spit out contemptuously. "Yeah, I'll believe it when it happens. When are you going to think of our future? Oh, and I suppose you still can't make it to the conference on Thursday?"

"Matt, I told you I can't come until after the last *Werther*. I'll meet you in Saratoga on Saturday. We'll have a nice weekend."

At that Matt rose from the table, set his dinner plate on the counter and strode upstairs signaling that this was his last word on the subject. "For tonight, anyway," Clemence thought.

****

Clemence checked her watch nervously for the hundredth time. There was no sign of the bus for Saratoga. though she had been waiting anxiously for forty-five minutes. Two completely full coaches had passed her and the others who stood trying to flag them down at the highway stop. The dispatcher had assured her that a third would be on the way in another half hour. Clemence had called Matt's cell, and as usual it had rung endlessly before he picked up. He seemed seriously miffed at her predicament.

"Damn it, Clemence! I'm on my way to the station, and you're not even on the bus! We're going to miss our brunch at the polo club."

"Well, I'm sorry. It's not my fault. I've been waiting for almost an hour. I just hope there's a seat on the next one. I'll call you as soon as I get on. Please answer."

"Great!" Matt grunted and clicked off.

Just as he did, the blue and white Adirondack Trailways coach slid to a stop and opened the doors. "Only one seat left," barked the driver.

First in line, Clemence breathed a sigh of relief, gathered up her duffle and her briefcase, and climbed aboard. The unoccupied seat was way in the back on the window side. She lurched down the aisle, hoisted her duffle to the overhead, and thanked the young man who rose to let her in.

"Crowded," he smiled apologetically.

"Hmnn, glad I'm on," Clemence replied. "My husband is meeting me in Saratoga." She pulled out her cell and hastily dialed Matt, who miraculously answered on the first ring.

"I'm on my way. I got the last seat," Clemence chirped as cheerily as she could.

"Great! Sorry I was pissy before. So I guess I'll see you at noon at the bus station. I'm driving across 323 in Vermont right now."

"OK, hon. See you soon."

She hung up and settled back in her seat. She pretended to watch the scenery roll by on the Thruway, but her glance kept creeping over to the young man beside her. He was in his early twenties, slim, clean-cut with an attractive head of thick, well-shaped dark hair. But what really caught her eye was the magazine he was reading.

"*American Choral Arts*? Are you a singer?" she queried.

He looked up surprised. “Yeah, I’m a tenor, actually. I’m on my way to a choir competition in Montreal. I’ve got a couple of solos.”

“How wonderful!” Clemence replied. “I work for a tenor, myself.”

The young man’s eyes sparked with interest. He offered his hand. “I’m Andrew Hillis. Pleased to meet you.”

“Clemence,” she murmured. “Same here. So where did you study?’

I just finished a Bachelor of Music at Carnegie Mellon, and I’m applying to grad schools, but I’m going to take a semester off and do some auditions, to get some experience.”

“What’s your repertoire?” Clemence persisted.

“Lyric stuff now – Mozart, Gounod, arts songs and oratorio.”

“Perfect,” Clemence encouraged. “Keep it light and go slowly. You’ve got lots of time.”

“Are you a manager?”

“No, I do special projects – research, writing, media.”

Andrew nodded appreciatively, and then after a brief pause, he summoned his courage and asked, "So which tenor do you work for?"

"Derek Howe."

"Oh, my goodness!" Andrew exclaimed. "Then you are Clemence Marguy! I loved your Heldentenor book. You really know the voice! I've read everything you've ever written."

Clemence stared speechlessly at the young man whose face had lit up with delight as he loosed a torrent of enthusiasm. "Derek Howe is one of my idols. If ever I could sound like him, especially in lieder – " Andrew didn't finish.

"Yes, he is an extraordinary lieder singer," Clemence agreed.

"Can I ask you something? What's it like to work for him. Is he as amazing as he seems?"

Clemence was silent for several beats. She rejected the platitudes that leapt to her lips. Instead, she looked Andrew directly in the eyes and said as quietly and dispassionately as she could, "It has its moments to be sure, but for the most part I'm always invisible. I'm always an assistant."

Before Andrew could process her candor, his cell phone rang. He flashed Clemence a contrite look for interrupting. “Hi, Mom. Yeah, I’m on my way to Montreal for the competition. We’re in New York now. I’ve got to change in Albany.”

Clemence turned away and stared out the window, trying not to eavesdrop. For what seemed an eternity Andrew chatted amiably with his mother. Clemence caught only snatches of familiar banalities until she heard Andrew signal a goodbye.

“I’ve got to go, Mom. I’m almost at my stop. Mom, do you know whom I just met? Yes, right here on the bus! Clemence Marguy!” Apparently, the name meant nothing to Andrew’s mother for he continued animatedly, “Remember the Heldentenor book I read last year?” Whether this credit did anything to jolt Andrew’s mother’s memory, Clemence could not say because the young man was quickly signing off. “Gotta go, Mom. Love you.”

He turned ruefully to Clemence just as the driver’s voice over the loudspeaker announced, “Albany. Five minutes. Change for Montreal.”

“I’m sorry. I would have liked to talk longer,” he said.

Clemence smiled and, reaching into her purse, pulled out a business card and handed it to the young man. It read *Clemence Marguy, Personal Assistant to Derek Howe.* "Let's stay in touch. I can probably get you a ticket for one of Derek's concerts in New York, if you like."

"That would be amazing!" Andrew grinned as he stood up and offered another handshake. "It's been such a pleasure to meet you, Ms. Marguy," he added politely.

"Clemence," she corrected. "I'll watch for your name some time soon."

Collecting his clumsy duffle bag from the overhead, Andrew flashed another boyish grin and headed down the aisle as the bus swung into the bay at the Albany station. Clemence waited until Andrew had disembarked. He stood on the platform for a few seconds finding his bearings and then raised his hand in a shy farewell. Clemence waved back.

As the Trailways coach backed out and headed again for the Thruway, Clemence reached for her phone. "Hey, Matt," she sang into the receiver. "I'm almost there. We're just leaving Albany."

"Great. I'm in the rental car at the depot here in Saratoga. It's a black Camry. See you soon, sweetie." Clemence thought she heard a click.

"Matt, are you still there?"

"Yeah, what?"

"Matt, I just had the most extraordinary experience on the bus –"

# GOODBYE

Chantal Laurence fluttered her heavy eyelids open but left her head resting against the train window as New Haven slipped by. In little more than an hour she would be in New York City. It seemed like ages since she had set foot in the city, let alone a theatre there. "A lifetime ago," she thought, the familiar melancholy rising up in her throat.

It had been her home – their home, that is – when Lee had been alive. Not literally, of course, because she and Leander had lived across the river in Hoboken, but they spent all their working days and most of their leisure nights in Gotham. Their friends were there; the theatres and concert halls, opera and ballet held them in sirens' thrall. For Chantal, who had been an educator and later became an arts critic and journalist who had traveled the international scene, New York was still her epicenter - that is, until 9/11, which shook her confidence to the very core. Somehow, it was as if her city, through no fault of its own, had betrayed her by being vulnerable, and she, too, had become weak and assailable.

The move to Maine a few years later seemed to make perfect sense to the Laurences. Lee was close to retirement, and Chantal's gig with the *Village Voice* was drying up. It was time for a change. Time to take things slower, breathe the fresh air and find their center again.

And they did. For ten glorious months life began anew for Chantal and Leander until Lee stepped onto that treadmill one winter day and embarked on a journey without a return.

That catastrophic day now seemed eons ago; so much else had crowded into the chaos of Chantal's life in the intervening four years. Little by little, she had arduously reclaimed the shards of her existence, though anytime an unruly sliver broke away, it pierced her heart anew.

Her head hurt, and it made her tired to think about it. She rubbed her eyes and straightened in her seat. She was exhausted, and she still had an evening at the theatre ahead of her. Perhaps, if the train weren't late, she could catch a quick nap at the hotel before the 8:00 p.m. curtain.

"Naps are good," Dr. Blake had reassured her "– not a sign of weakness." Chantal hated any hint of illness. Her recent brush with a breast tumor had been enough to rock her precarious sense of stoic strength. It had been benign, thank goodness, and excised, but Chantal could not even let herself travel beyond that thought to the what if.

In the months after Leander had died, she would have gladly followed him, but at first it was Ruffian, her Newf girl, who needed her, and now she had a book to finish – her novel about Lee and their marriage was a sacred promise – and then she was negotiating a contract for a biography of her old friend, the famous tenor Paul Hochhalter, and she was reviewing again.

"Not tonight, though," she smiled to herself. Tonight's trip to Broadway was strictly for pleasure and to surprise another old friend, her former drama student James – Tristan James Torveig, as he now used his full name on stage. For the last six months he had been starring in a new musical which had been built around his considerable talents, and tonight was the last performance. She'd have come before, but work and life kept throwing up roadblocks.

Well, at least here she was. Chantal sighed contentedly, reaching for her small overnight and briefcase as the train rolled onto Track 2 at Penn Station.

A dash uptown to the Empire, a quick check-in, brief nap, shower and change into something dressier than the plain business suit in which she usually discharged her critic's duties, and Chantal was on her way in a cab down to the Neil Simon Theatre.

She felt the familiar adrenalin surge as she hurried under the marquee where Torveig's infectious smile beamed down at her and then into the theatre and down the aisle to her fifth-row-center seat. For a minute she imagined Leander would step over her to claim the empty seat beside, as he had for every student show she had directed and for so many of the professional ones she had covered. Instead, a paunchy, fiftyish, balding man, excusing himself, clumsily made his way past her just as the house lights dimmed.

The orchestra struck up the bright opening chords as Chantal settled back in her seat. Closing nights were always hard – as an ex-director and performer, she knew that. James must have been taken aback by the decision to end the run. He had received raves, but the critics had found the story of a runaway teenager turned charismatic conman too slick and predictable, and they appeared to miss the sheer joie de vivre in the music and lyrics, not to mention Torveig's dazzling singing. Chantal had played the album so often in the last few months that she had to buy a second copy.

The evening sped by. Chantal couldn't take her eyes off her Tristan. Not only did he seem so dashingly handsome – that blond hair swept back with flawless perfection, the flashing, dimpled smile, his trim athletic physique, and what a dancer he had become – but, most of all, now he appeared to her to be supremely confident.

In high school he had always been most at home on the stage. She had recognized from the first she had taught him that the theatre was his calling – well, theatre and music because could James – Tristan (she had to get used to his new persona) ever sing! Even then she knew this was a voice! That's why she had pushed him so hard to train it. And she had won that battle with the help of his parents in his junior year. She had accompanied him to his Juilliard audition and was thrilled when he made the pre-college voice program.

When he graduated from high school, Tristan had left Juilliard for NYU, where he chose to major in musical theatre, but he took with him the foundations that made him the vocal phenomenon he was today: that gorgeous, golden, lyric tenor sound and the range! What was that high note he had just floated?

As the applause swelled, Chantal came back into herself. She struggled to remain in the present.

The next few numbers raced by while she focused with pride on the subtle force and charisma of Tristan's acting. He was living his role, tonight more than ever.

It was time for the eleven-o'clock showpiece. For Tristan's character the game was over. It was his time to say "Goodbye." The orchestra held its breath for a moment before launching softly into the song.

*It's my happy ending*, Tristan's clean, sweet tenor shaped the words with a hint of a tremolo.

"He's close to tears," Chantal thought, and in truth so was she. She knew that look – his eyes narrowed tightly, hoping to squeeze away the drops that were forming; the dimpled chin trembled ever so slightly.

"You can do it, Tristan," a voice whispered in Chantal's head. "This is your moment. This and only this."

*Now it's time to say goodnight*. The orchestra began to soar. The audience's energy seemed to surge across the footlights, as Tristan poured out his soul. *Goodbye to lives that I don't own – Goodbye - Goodbye – Goodbye*! The last clarion note was a cri de coeur that shattered the house and dimmed the spotlight. For a split second there was a breathless, stunned silence, a moment of suspended awe, and then it happened. With a deafening roar the audience rose to its feet and began to cheer.

Professional though he was, Tristan was having trouble holding his pose. His arm pumped in the air began to quiver; his chest started to heave, and he surrendered his body to his emotion. Tristan dropped his arm and let his head sink onto his chest, a humble thank you. As if by inspired instinct, the spotlight man brought up his lamp, creating an arc around the actor, and the applause turned to stomping. There was no possibility for the orchestra to continue.

Slowly, Tristan lifted his head and his blue eyes reached out to the back of the balcony. The tears rolled down his cheeks, and he let them. His shoulders shook, but his smile dazzled. And still the audience cheered, “Bravo!”

“Bravo,” Chantal chimed in. She surprised herself. As a critic, she never allowed herself that sort of public display, but this was different. And it was just then, as her voice had joined the chorus, that Tristan’s glance seemed to find her. His smile broadened; he gulped, and ever so imperceptibly, he inclined his head in her direction. Chantal’s knees seemed to jelly, and she gripped the seat back in front of her for support.

How long it took for the waves of applause to ebb and Tristan to regain his composure, Chantal could not tell. But all at once the orchestra was again playing and Tristan had vanished back into the drama.

The wild demonstrations continued at the curtain calls. There were speeches and thank yous and flowers and more tears. And then it was over – a transforming chapter in a boy's young life closed, one of the many endings that shape an actor's experience.

But what an ending! "It had a magic and mystery of its own," Chantal thought as she made her way to the stage door. She pulled out her press credentials for the porter, but without looking he waved her on.

"Mr. Torveig's dressing room is the first on the left," he instructed.

When Chantal knocked and then entered, Tristan was standing bare-chested in his slacks, a towel around his neck, surrounded by a crowd of admirers. He was signing autographs, making polite small talk, and smiling cordially. Chantal installed herself quietly in the back corner of the room, observing the people. She recognized a record executive from EMI chatting with a woman who must be Tristan's manager. It was a few minutes before that swell dispersed and Tristan was able to look up. He spied her and made his way through the lingerers. He opened his arms and enfolded Chantal in a bear hug.

"It is you! You made it!" he beamed. "Why didn't you call me? I'd have sent you a ticket."

"I wasn't sure I'd be able to make it. Things have been a little dicey lately," Chantal apologized.

"Yeah, I am so sorry about Mr. Laurence," Tristan murmured, still holding her hand.

Chantal nodded solemnly. "Yes, thanks, it has been a difficult time. But it is SO good to see you!"

"I thought maybe you would have come to the press opening in the spring."

"I tried, but I wasn't on the list. My byline isn't what it used to be. Maine is not New York and regional critics . . ."

"I didn't know," he said earnestly. "I'll make sure that doesn't happen again."

The room had almost emptied; only the manager and the EMI representative were left, smiling politely but expectantly at Tristan.

“Susan, can you give me a moment alone?” Tristan said softly. The manager nodded with a forced smile and guided her guest out of the room. “Sure thing, Tris. We’ll wait outside.”

“Thanks.” He waited for the door to close. “Sit, please, Mrs. Laurence.”

“Chantal, please. And I see you are Tristan James now,” she smiled. “It has a ring.”

“How long has it been since we last got together?” he asked. “Before I went on my first tour? When I left NYU?”

“Years, yes. We moved and then . . .” Chantal faltered. “But I’ve followed everything you’ve done. And I have been so proud.”

“I really lost it tonight,” Tristan whispered, shaking his head.

Chantal reached out and placed her hand over his. “Yes, you did, and you know what? You gave one of the bravest, most honest, most beautiful performances I have ever experienced.”

“I felt so exposed, so absolutely naked.”

“Without the mask,” she queried gently. “Never apologize for an emotion that is real. The stage is a place where you must always tell the truth."

Tristan smiled appreciatively. "Thanks. That means a lot to me. I wouldn't be here without you – Chantal," he hesitated at using her given name.

"You wouldn't be here without yourself," she corrected.

"Remember *Brigadoon* and *Death of a Salesman*, and *West Side Story*? They were the best experiences of my high school years. You gave me the skills and the drive I needed to go for a career."

"You had a special gift; of so many talented students I've taught, you had that something extra. That's why I pushed so hard."

"I remember you kicked my butt, and I deserved it. I remember coming to you to say I had been elected captain of the football team and I'd love to have the lead, but I would have to miss some rehearsals, and you were as adamant as I have ever seen you."

"I told you I couldn't make an exception for you, no matter how wonderful your audition was – that the play was too demanding, and it needed all your energy."

“And then you dropped the real bombshell. You wouldn’t cast me as Tony if I didn’t agree to take voice lessons – that it was time to take it seriously and make a commitment to music and theatre or to move on.”

Chantal nodded. “I purposely picked a challenging show to have you and Ben and John and Beth stretch yourselves. I knew you could do it if you really wanted to. And your parents were super, weren’t they?” she added.

“They came up with the money for the lessons, and they were strict with me about practicing,” he agreed, scrunching up his eyes and lips again – that telltale sign that the tears weren’t entirely gone. “It scares me to think what if I had been stubborn and not listened to you.”

“You listened to your own inner voice; it was too strong to disregard. You just needed permission,“ she smiled, “and a sharp kick to act on what you already knew was true.”

“How did you know I wouldn’t opt for being popular and staying with football - the suburban New York high school dream – after all?” Irony tinged his voice.

“I didn’t know, but I felt it.”

Tristan bowed his head for a moment and said with a shy awkwardness, “ I owe you so much, Mrs. Laurence.”

“Nice of you to say, but you owe no one but yourself. Promise. Always be as committed as you were tonight. And it’s Chantal,” she twitted, rising to her feet, “Tristan James Torveig,” she said with teasing emphasis. “Susan is probably getting impatient.”

He acquiesced apologetically, as she started for the door. He stopped her in her tracks. “I’m headed to LA for a movie.”

“I heard. That’s wonderful!”

“I’ll see you back in New York,” he offered.

“I hope so,” Chantal managed. “It’s my turn to say goodbye.”

She stepped back into the dressing room and held out her arms, expecting a hug. Instead, Tristan bent over and, with courtly deference, kissed one of her outstretched hands. As he straightened to his full height, she caught a glimpse of another furtive tear. Her glance was warm, but unyielding. Chantal looked deep into those blue eyes.

Tristan sighed softly. “Then goodbye for now.” And with a luminous smile he let that tear fall.

CPSIA information can be obtained at www.ICGtesting.com
Printed in the USA
BVOW03s0440180214

345226BV00005B/10/P

9 781467 597852